SECRETS
NEW SCOTTISH WRITING

SECRETS

New Scottish Writing

EDITED BY JANICE GALLOWAY

The Scotsman & Orange
Short Story Collection 2005

Polygon

First published in Great Britain in 2005 by Polygon
an imprint of Birlinn Ltd,
West Newington House, 10 Newington Road,
Edinburgh EH9 1QS

www.birlinn.co.uk

Introduction © Janice Galloway, 2005
Stories © the Contributors, 2005

Typeset in Minion by Palimpsest Book Production Limited,
Polmont, Stirlingshire
Printed and bound in Great Britain by
Creative Print & Design, Ebbw Vale, Wales

A CIP record for this book is
available from the British Library

ISBN 1 904598 37 4

The publisher acknowledges subsidy from

 Scottish
Arts Council

towards the publication of this volume

CONTENTS

Introduction

JANICE GALLOWAY

'Although it must be a thousand years ago that I sat in a class in story writing at Stanford, I remember the experience very clearly. I was bright-eyed and bushy-brained and prepared to absorb the secret formula for writing good short stories, even great short stories. This illusion was cancelled very quickly. The only way to write a good short story, we were told, is to write a good short story.' John Steinbeck

'Writing isn't just telling stories. It's exactly the opposite. It's everything all at once. It's the telling of a story, the absence of a story. It's telling a story through its absence.' Marguerite Duras
Writing short stories is a terrifying business. Ask anyone who knows. I have quoted Duras and Steinbeck because I love them and what they have to say is so to-the-point, but really, you could take your pick. Alternatively, you could let me take it for you.

Franz Kafka, a man forever hoist with his own metaphor of a human being turned into a giant insect, suffered agonies of guilt about not working hard enough or long enough, and saw the business of writing his stories as 'drawing words as if out of the empty air'. 'If I capture one,' he confided to his diary, 'then I have just this one alone, and all the toil must begin anew.' The incomparable Virginia Woolf, who would today be harassed to call her stories novels for the greater good of her publisher's sales figures, spoke of drawing ideas up as from the bottom of a well, with great effort and no little anxiety before the meticulous business of applying craft to those 'fished out' ideas even begins. New Zealander Katherine Mansfield chimes clearly with these sentiments, and adds a little of her own on the subject of the relentless need to edit, revise, rework: 'Tidied all my papers. Tore up and ruthlessly destroyed much, which always gives the greatest satisfaction.' Katherine Anne Porter, the Texan author who won a Pulitzer prize for her *Collected Stories*, spoke of the requirement to spend time 'simmering' with a story which could not, she asserted, be driven by craft or even by so-called 'writers' intuition': 'I don't believe in intuition. When you get sudden flashes of perception, it is just the brain working faster than usual. But you've been getting ready to know it for a long time, and when it comes, you feel you've known it always. There's no other way.' In other words, the story comes, if it comes, when it comes; the author has no real control over the pace of events. Patience, it seems, is a primary requirement. And there's more. Here comes the relentless nature of the beast.

Evan Connell, quoted by Raymond Carver, said he knew he was finished with a short story when he found himself going through it and taking out commas, then going through the story again and putting commas back in the same places. 'That's all we have, finally, the words,' says Carver, 'and they better be the right ones, with the punctuation in the right places so they can best say what they are meant to say. If the words are heavy with the writer's own unbridled emotions, or they are imprecise and inaccurate for some other reason, the reader's eye will slide right over them and nothing will be achieved.'

Difficult, frustrating, demanding, elusive, painstaking, awkward, uncompromising – and we're not done yet. Even if you find the time and the persistence, even if you craft your hardest, shape your phrases into as robust and beautiful an arrangement as you know how; even if you manage to make the story resonate like crystal, there is no guarantee (how could there be?) that people will read it as you intend. 'All my stories,' said the incomparable Flannery O'Connor, 'are about the action of grace on a character who is not very willing to support it, but most people think of these stories as hard, hopeless and brutal. It's always a shock.'

Duras, Mansfield, O'Connor, Porter, Steinbeck, Kafka, Woolf and Carver, mistresses and masters of the form, are an impressive enough roster of confidants. I could add Rudyard Kipling, Shirley Jackson, Guy de Maupassant and Anton Chekhov, Edgar Allan Poe and Alice Munro, James Joyce, James Kelman and Jackie Kay, Charles Dickens and Grace Paley, Fyodor Dostoevsky and Jorge Luis Borges and Angela Carter and Gertrude Stein and Oscar Wilde and Hogg and Spark and Hardy and Hemingway and – but I won't. The message is probably loud enough already.

It is also hard to ignore the fact that short stories are not cash-cows. Novels earn more in terms of advances and are more attractive to publishers – and here we're talking whole collections. In terms of individual stories, fewer magazines and periodicals publish them at all, and the demand on the writer to be impressive enough to capture the attention of those that do is consequently greater.

What, then, is the attraction? Why write the buggers at all? That, contrarily enough, is easy to answer. And since he started us off, Steinbeck's the man to do it. 'After many years,' he confesses, 'to start a story still scares me to death. I will go so far as to say that the writer who is not scared is happily unaware of the remote and tantalising majesty of the medium. I have written a great many stories and I still don't know how to go about it except to write it and take my chances.'

That's it. The wish to 'take one's chances' with the 'tantalising majesty of the medium' itself, challenges intact, is the draw.

It is traditional, when talking of the short story, to elaborate upon that notion of 'medium'; the usual assertions of less being more, the thrill of the smaller canvas, the requirement for characters to simply be without preamble or vast stretches of white page to go, but this is merely to elaborate upon the obvious, to restate that the thing about the short story is its shortness. Sure it is: impact, import and resolution in one sweep. More intriguing to expand upon is the 'majesty' part of the quotation. I suggest that majesty rests largely in a quality the short story shares with all literary art, but different types of writing, at least arguably, deliver that quality in different ways. Added to the story's particular demands and contours, this quality lends a particular piquancy and allure. And that quality is transcendence.

If a fine novel is a whole exhibition, a fine short story is a single picture. It is a picture, however, by Julia Margaret Cameron or Weegee, by Diane Arbus or Cartier-Bresson, a picture where the glimpse suggests what came before, what is yet to come, the wider landscape stretching out into infinite space.

And finding the viewpoint, the moment, as unarguably as is the case with the photographer, is above all a matter of waiting and of precision. It imposes a requirement to observe steadily, to catch what images and connections are already coming together beneath the ordinary appearance of things as you work. By this I do not mean that one must wait for the plot to unfold (though this may happen too – some writers report the oddest things happening as their characters 'take off' as if with minds of their own). I mean one must wait for enlightenment of a kind. The question here is not what's the story? but what is the story trying to tell me? What is it, after all, that I mean to say? This enlightenment is not a matter of craft, a matter of refining your characters or setting or the naturalness of your dialogue or any other teachable thing: it is a matter of self-trust, of tiny tics of understanding. It is a slow apprehension of what this story means beyond the story itself.

Of course, one must refine and apply a full measure of technical skill; one must attend to the detail of consistency and readability of the whole. But it is only when the writer can see a wider context that they offer something the reader can experience as theirs too. That is what Duras means when she argues that the story is 'everything all at once'. A complete world, convincingly peopled; something fresh made from the everyday of course, of course. But more than this. 'The telling of a story, the absence of a story. It's telling a story through its absence.' That's all there is to it.

Competitions, of course, don't always help this process. In place of 'writing everything at once', for example, the competition invariably sets up a 'theme' and, more understandably, a word-length. Instead of allowing the story to emerge as it must, the competition writer must drive the elements of their story towards a pre-set destination, which, if my earlier assertions about patient waiting are true, is tantamount to demanding the story be thought and written inside out. How easy is that likely to be?

This book, then, with its theme of 'secrets' set a very particular and tough series of tasks with a tender goal – to have that story do its work by being published and read by a wider public and the possibility, in a money-starved genre, of winning some money to keep writing. Over 1,200 people took their chances and they had their work cut out. The vast majority of those, of course, fell. The primary killer was endings. Some stories began splendidly but refused to keep going, as though the word-limit had disallowed the original ambition to keep pumping; some did not manage the hurdle of a satisfactory ending that meant more than the cessation of the plot; some reined themselves in so much they were too 'tight' for the reader to unlace the ending's meaning so the story died of asphyxia. A great many, alas, resorted to 'twists' or relied too heavily on hammering home the 'secret' contained within, so the reader had little to do but pick up the author's punch-line at the close, which is about as deadly as it gets. Some came very close indeed, but just were not strong enough, at least in this editorial panel's opinion, at the last jump. The thirteen survivors you now hold in your hands and I trust you will be impressed by at least their tenacity. We hope they will speak clearly, cleanly and memorably to you. We believe all of those printed here have a something to say, and all at least strive to reach beyond themselves with what that something is. There is range and choice enough for at least one transcendental gem to fall into your lap.

You may glimpse it in one of the many stories we received about the hidden lives of children and adolescents. It may be set in Holland or Bali, in Soweto, Aberdeen or Baghdad. You may uncover it alongside the abandoned Burnhouse Estate baby or in the playful nips and tucks of one final conversation with God; on beaches, by rock pools; in the words of a slick-talking PI, the silence of a mermaid doll or in the sound of birdsong to a near-sightless child. From Derek Robertson's tightly crafted 'A Softer Devil', where a lonely 15-year-old begins to find an account of himself, to Nicolas McGregor's weary gumshoe on the psychiatrist's couch in 'The Martha Day Affair'; from Ewan Gault's 'The Beast', a raw-edged tale of abandonment and barely-acknowledged grief, to sick-at-heart Mr Em's Christmas drink with the girls in Frances Watt's atmospheric 'Over the Counter'; from Anne Morrison's beautifully modulated tale of girls fishing and finding more than they can yet understand at 'Gorilla Rock' to the multi-layered depths of Kirstin Zhang's 'Enemy Within', where Akbar, cheating death, his wife and his neighbours, discovers he can't lie to himself; all are jewel-cased here.

In addition, there are a trio of commissions from three collection-scarred professionals, all struggling themselves against the same odds and coming through with the kind of grace, power and style that often merits the absurd adjective 'effortless' as its due praise. Ali Smith gives a finely pared-down warning in the uncomfortably resonant 'I know something you don't know'; Bernard MacLaverty finely pares back layers of cultural and sexual mores to something darker, even, than grief in 'The Wedding Ring'; and Jackie Kay tilts heart, head and the very windows to the wider world in a 65-carat fine-cut diamond of a story, 'Blinds'.

All that waiting, you see, can have its rewards, for writer and reader alike. Even Kafka, that most fretful of a fretful breed, knew it.

'You do not need to leave your room,' he wrote in a moment of rare joy. 'Remain sitting at your table and listen. Do not even listen, simply wait. Do not even wait, be quiet, still and solitary. The world will freely offer itself to you to be unmasked, it has no choice, it will roll in ecstasy at your feet.'

Now who wouldn't want to try their chances for that?

Imprint

JOHN ABERDEIN

He got off the bus from Northfield at Causewayend, the smoke adhering to his hair from the upper deck, where he chose to sit so he could read some tome, in this case Camus' *Plague*. The lower deck was usually jammed, and you had to give up your seat to any wifie over fifty, specially with bags, or any dodderer clasping a ferruled crook or stick. *Do not alight from the bus while it is still moving.* They called it *alighting*. He jumped from the open platform early: the joy of his heels' jolt, the rubbery soles then slamming to a halt.

It was a wide windy hole, Causewayend, he could feel the winds jostle there, a steadyish sea breeze from Nelson Street, where he'd gone to school; but also frequent gusts along West North Street, with the whiff of the lodging-house; plus the odd buffet coming down Gallowgate. When had the last guy been hanged in town, he couldn't mind, not all that long. Not publicly though, the world had grown genteel. *The Granite City*. So genteel! You made no impact: the very stone, the architecture, was against you. At least in Pompeii some gestures got melted into the lava, at least in Hiroshima you left a shadow on brick, the moment you vaporised. But Aberdeen was adamant: folk were its architecture's secrets.

Coming across the roundabout he saw Chris, Chrissie. Chrisaline Farquharson. He wished she had been a little ahead, so he could have caught her up and surprised her, but instead he waited, swung awkwardly and waited, trying to fashion a thing to say.

She had on that black shortie PVC coat – all the rage down Carnaby Street, though not many north girls had one – her bunched hair snug inside her upturned collar. She had a battered briefcase under her arm which didn't really go, being brown, but she carried it off. Nearly across from the roundabout she glanced up at him and tilted her head, and he could feel his quick colour. He wouldn't try to be witty, stutter over it, just ask how she was. But then she would think *too straight, not interested*—

– Hiya—she said.

– Hi—

He felt a nameless scent swoop over him, heading to Varsity for the sophisticated sniffers.

– Big Library day—?

– No, she said. I'm for this Greek seminar, chance it anyway.

– Me ditto, amazing. Crete, though, isn't it?

– Hope so—

– Great.

They walked almost together as the way narrowed and steepened, *Spital* they called it. Peem often had to hop down on to the roadway as they edged past cardboard boxes and buckets. For it was bucket day in the Spital, and the grey alloy buckets the corporation insisted on stood on the pavement, each with its strong, fluted, integrated lid that couldn't blow off. The last thing you wanted in Aberdeen was any looseness and rubbish spilling.

– They've found more oil, then, said Peem.

It wasn't the greatest chat-up line.

– Have they—? Who?

– I think, said Peem.

He hopped down once more amongst the leaves and cobbles.

– Nice old bag.

– I beg— O, that!

– Makes you look all academic.

No, it precisely bloody didn't.

– Ta, fat chance. My Dad's. He doesn't need it. Sermons are shorter these days. And the lectures.

– Is he a—?

– Bar the ones he gives me, of course.

– Ha, said Peem.

– *Satan's Smoke, Beelzebub o the Booze—*

– I know, he said. *Auld Clootie in Your Very Dumpling.*

– His latest, of course – *Manifold Evils of the Pill—*

She glanced as he slipped behind.

He's nearly gone over his ankle on the kerb.

They climbed round the next twist of the Spital. Three police were strung across the road, with their backs to them, holding half-hung hessian sacking. A dark beige ambulance stood with its doors open. Their legs slowed as they came up.

Peem felt a strange reverent voyeurism. A photographer was pointing his apparatus down, using one of those ridiculous cameras you had to put plates in. Then he slid out and replaced the unwieldy plate, shuffling to determine his next best angle. Not a soul had a word to utter.

Peem pointed as Chrisaline pointed. Two straggles of fluid had escaped, were still escaping, under the pitiful hessian curtaining, zagging their way free, tracking a way through the square-set cobbles. One line, watery, had attained the gutter. The other, darker, darker than blood should be, was too slow. Soft crimson glacier in the flecked glens of the granite.

– Foo did he land sae far oot? said the snapper.

– Sorry? said the sergeant.

– How did he land sae far oot, in the actual roadway? repeated the photographer.

– Search me, said the sergeant.

They looked up at the roof of the four-storey tenement that helped comprise the canyon of the Spital. There was an oblong hole where they were trying to replace a skylight. Exposed big rafters and thin sarking. But all around the hole, all around was just steep wet slates.

– Tae avoid aa them, I shouldna wonder, said the photographer. Bleedin railins.

The row of railings fencing the house, with piercy fleur-de-lys, was grim to think of from any height.

– See that guy in Torry last year? said a constable.

– Shut it, Chic!

A flurry of rain came on. It tried to dislodge the coagulate, towards a drain and the general sewage.

The rain woke the police to duty. There was no way through.

– No through way, said the sergeant.

They had to be doing with a different route to the University: three lefts and straight on. They had just rounded the first left, heading past the bus depot.

– Chrissie, who, what do you reckon—?

But this time it was she had fallen behind. One hand spread against the grey stone gable, she was bent double. He made an instinctive sort of move, then danced his feet clear. Slime after omeletty slime hit the asphalt walkway. That rancid smell of acidy spirits.

She tried to spit. She wiped at her mouth with the back of her hand.

– God, horrible, she said, on top of last night—

– Last night?

The moment she sought his arm he felt surges: disgust, desire, love, importance.

– Want a shot – look – take my hankie. Two wee slivers on your coat.

* * *

It made them late, of course, for Palio's seminar. They walked pretty slow, Chrisaline still kinda sick, squeamish, saying so. They stopped at a shop, but the man didn't sell water, and she didn't want gassy stuff. They walked on. Main thing again she slung her right through his left, leant almost, from time to time, in on him. They weren't suddenly going steady, he wasn't that big a fool, but for a first whatever-it-was, some feeling of each other, start, introduction, it was great: they would always remember.

– Shall we do another lap?

– Better go in, she said.

Not that it was good going in late, they gowked at you, and you never fully cottoned on. They were about to climb the steps to the ivied porch when a bronzed man in cream blouse, black bulky pantaloons and hard white knee-boots came down at an easy clip-clop towards them.

A fringe of black knots kicked at his brow.

– Are you students of me?

– Sorry we're—

– *Kali mera*, good morning, join me. I am heading out on a

good Nietzschean principle. Beyond the stuff of rooms, beyond civil.

Peem checked if the class was joining. Chrisaline disengaged her arm. A mild sun tried the Kilmarnock willow, static weeper in mid-quad.

– Now while we walk, let me say, let me indeed say—

Peem jostled closer. The stranger had a mountainous sweep of nose and a chin that bid bold to meet it.

– Let me confirm that we will have three seminars, of each two hours, plus a practical through lunchtime. You are—?

– O, Peem, Peem Endrie.

– And what makes you breathe? said the Cretan.

– Sorry?

– The most vital question of all. What makes you breathe!

– Involuntary, isn't it?

– Good, today we will change that. I will show you running.

– You'll show me running?

– And you, lady. You, like a gorge in spring—

– Chrisaline.

– Chrisaline, you have recently been crying. Did Peem make you so?

– No, we saw a man, fallen off a roof.

– Falling?

– Fallen. He was working— We think it was a man, it must have been.

– And now he is dead, no doubt. We men are fragile creatures, poorly designed for falling from roofs. So now we shall do what?

– We shall—? said Peem.

– Do what—? said Chrisaline.

– We shall seek in due time to discover why this man fell, this Icarus. What shabby artificer put him high in such danger.

– Shabby whatimifer? said Peem.

– But this way now, we must find a boundary, to test our limits.

– Excuse me, is there – where is – the rest of the class? said Chrisaline.

– No doubt coming.

– Cryptic, eh? said Peem to her, as they fell in behind.

She didn't have a need to put her arm back through.

Back in the Spital, they turned away from the town and its most recent tragedy, out past the massy Cathedral, down through the spacious park, along by the riverside, then briefly up onto King Street before crossing the Brig of Don. The Cretan looked back a couple of times. Chrisaline opened her coat, even in October. To be fair she did have on a red polo.

– Never mind falling off roofs. I have heard, said the Cretan, that dulling the brain is a national pastime.

– Sorry, what? said Peem.

– Dulling the brain, said the Cretan. I have heard it is a Scottish pastime.

– I suppose.

– I don't just refer to your stupid brown god, beer. I refer to deliberate ignorance, the wilful suppression of ideas. What do you—

– It'll be okay leaving this briefcase under the bridge, said Chrisaline, do you suppose? It's a bugger to carry.

She braked sideways down the bank, to stash the battered item in the shade of a pontoon.

– I don't know, said Peem. Most folk seem happy enough.

– Happy enough. A great ambition for the only species ever to be granted reflexive consciousness. Happy enough!

– Most other folk. Sometimes.

Chrisaline hadn't caught up yet. She shouted she'd gravel or something. The young man and the youth went back to her. She laid her left hand on the Cretan's corded forearm, then used her right to yank off and empty a slip-on.

– You have quite hard finger-skin, very.

– Guitar. You have to have.

– Classical?

– Anything but!

They left the road and the beach-path, and walked on top of the dunes, wending up and down in single file, not saying much, keeping it to themselves. Strange the incomer leading. Peem pondered reflexive consciousness, tracking Chrissie's rear.

They gradually came level with an old trawlerish wreck, red and sunk to its gunnels in the sand of the foreshore.

– The past cannot be so easily buried, said Palio Theodarakis over his shoulder. And it resurfaces if we try, like your Skara Brae, like our Knossos. What do you see here?

– Clapped-out trawler, said Chrisaline.

– Steamer surely, said Peem. That'll be her triple expansion boilers.

Way out to sea long pencils of swell were slanting in.

– Chrisaline, your reconstruction—?

– Don't know about reconstructions. They were probably fine and happy when they set out.

Peem could see the Cretan jib: that word again.

– Poseidon, intoned Peem, this far north—?

Dark lines of swell swung parallel to the beach.

– Or viciously drunk, said the Cretan. Perhaps he didn't hear tentative stuff.

– I can't remember it being on TV, said Chrisaline.

The first swell reared.

– TV is not ubiquitous, said the Cretan, yet. But when it is, we will know nothing, we will remember nothing. Now let us get some oxygen in the brain.

*　*　*

The dunes were spiked together with marram, a pointy grass that gave the shuffle of sea and land snapshots of stability. But wherever a plague of hares and hounds, or hurricane had issued, the marrams lost tenacity, the dune broke down to shifty chutes.

It was up one chute and down another, that the Cretan proposed that he and Peem now ran. Chrisaline said she would sit and watch, this time.

The Cretan pulled off two white leather boots, strong brown calves and feet emerging. He slackened his blouse and peeled it off. There was a slash mark across his left pap, deep in its time by the look, sealed across now. Livid, translucent, against his bronzeish skin.

She pointed to the hoop of black knots at his brow: abrupt pendula when he shook his head. The black pantaloons were staying on too.

Peem obviously felt he had less scope for divestment. He fiddled with the buckle of his navy cords, then just hoicked off his Marksies brogues and lemon brilon socks. Black brogues had not been designed for running on dunes, and never for those socks.

Palio offered his hand.

– You lead, I'll follow, said Peem.

– You will try, said the Cretan.

The first few steps were awkward, easy. Further up, even with driving rhythm, it would be tough, unremittingly tough, each cramped step upwards betrayed by a splaying scuffle. So it was simple. Either you drove with fists clenched, really drove, or there would be no progress. No simulacrum of technique, but only desire, could carry you upward.

Although as it steepened Peem dug the harder, the iron Cretan inched ahead. Pumped up onto the humped skyline, they swung left, jogged slack-limbed, then hang-dog skedaddled down again.

– How easy is that! said Chrisaline.

– Bast-ards! breathed Peem, careful to use the anonymous plural.

– One minute recovery, said the singular Cretan.

They were to do what he was pleased to call *sets*, a single run followed by three in a row, then five then three then one again.

– We call it a *pyramid*, said Palio.

– Call it what you b-well like, said Peem.

– A good name—

– For slaves, *pyramid* was never a good name, said Peem.

– I concede your excellent historical point, said the Cretan. However, at this point in history, shall we say since Rilke, the task is to take all ideas and phenomena and remake them inwardly, for ourselves.

– Rilke? said Peem. Come again?

– Indeed, said the Cretan.

He set off driving: they did the three.

– German poet, said Chrisaline, wasn't he. Lived solo in castles and wrote sonnets and elegies, cribbed from angels.

– Nice work – if you can get it, said Peem.

– It is good to simplify, said the Cretan, as long as we are all aware – of the infinite spiritual pain of what lies beneath.

– I forgot to mention, said Chrisaline, that he had a string of high-born ladies who kept him—

– In their keep, punned Peem.

– So there you have it, said Palio. Four thousand years of European history, recapitulated from slave to patroness, from embalming of the body for eternal life, to the drive – Rilke's drive – to save the crumbling moments of the world, make everything inward.

– And our drive here, up this blood-curdling hill? said Peem.

– Will be for you, the first infinitely memorable thing that we do together. Come now, next set.

They did the five, outwardly, inwardly, and threw themselves on the sand.

– What is this course called again? said Chrisaline. It's a bit brisker than Old English.

– This course – is founded on – a mistake in communication—

– Take your time, said Chrisaline.

– Between the fine establishment – of Aberdeen – and the University of Crete in Heraklion.

– Mistake?

– Yes, the request was conveyed principally – by phone. Apparently your Arts Faculty Professor asked for a suitable young lecturer to give a brief course on – *Reassessing Cretan Ideas*. My Professor, who has more wax in his left ear than Icarus had on his wings, thought he said *Reassessing Creaking Ideas* – and, as the young blood in the Department, he had no hesitation in passing the request to me. All the rest of our communications with Aberdeen seemed to have centred on travel, domicile, timetable, stipend, the impedimenta of my brief non-tenure.

– Has nobody twigged? said Chrisaline.

– *I* have, as you say, *twigged*. What can a big tree do but go woodenly on. You asked earlier where the class might be.

– And—?

– And it is time for our three, Mr Endrie.

The breeze was rising. They did the three.

– I believe – that you two – were the only ones sufficiently seduced by the Minoan to enrol. However, when our secret gets out – if it gets out – that the course I have prepared is not *Cretan Ideas* but *Ideas That Creak* – and subtitled *The Cradle of Tomorrow* – then I think we can hope for better things.

– O, good, said Peem. As long as somebody else has to creak up this b-awful sandhill.

– That breeze, said Chrisaline.

– A fast one to finish, said the Cretan.

– My thighs are like lead, said Peem.

– When they are like plutonium, they will be the thighs of the future.

They did the one. Peem even tried to pass him, in a blur of imprinting.

Sprawling down a last loose chute, momentum carried them on to the long mangle of grey surf, where each flung the remainder of his raiment off, and plunged gratefully in.

Chrisaline plucked and plucked at the neck of her polo. Breathing the warmth between her breasts, she kept watching, at a distance, the two naked men.

Tower of Babel

ANDREW ALEXANDER

Our man's name is Maurice Chapman. This, however, is not his real name. He has not used his real name for several years, it is not even something that he has heard spoken in that time. In his line of business, real names are not the done thing.

Maurice is standing on his balcony, leaning against the guard rail. He wears a bathrobe, although he has not bathed in days. He is smoking a cigarette, his third since he came outside, with inadvertent ostentation: inhaling determinedly, wearily exhaling, as smokers do when introspective. He has been staring out across the river, watching the moonlight flicker across its darkness like static on a television screen, his eyelids drooped, his body ready for sleep. The city has been quiet beneath him, much of the city is entirely dark, power lost in another series of brownouts: no cars have moved across the bridges daisy-chained between the banks, no people have walked in the streets below. I am, he muses, almost entirely alone in the world right now.

Following this moment of reflection, his belly pressed hard against the rail, Maurice sees himself jumping. Clearly imagines himself taking off his bathrobe, clambering up over the guard rail, steadying himself on the outer lip of his balcony, arms behind him on the rail, bending his knees and leaning forward like a diver – then leaping out into the darkness, the wind ripping against his body as he plummets, all twelve floors, to the ground. It is always like this, leaving a place for the last time, knowing that you will never return. Thinking about taking your own life, surely not unnatural, this fascination with irreversible change.

Something normal people must think about, once in a while, when caught in the slipstream of a bus or a train shuttling past, gripped for a moment with the thought that they could have stepped into its path only a moment before, brought it all to an end.

Or, perhaps not, he deliberates. With all he has seen, he is far from normal, certainly too far. He takes a final drag on his cigarette, he places it on the rail, and flicks it out into the darkness with his index finger and thumb, following its arc as it falls. He sips from the tumbler, sluicing the last of the arak around his mouth, the aniseed burning at his tongue. Looking briefly at the glass, octagonal and heavy in his hand, he hurls it out over the balcony after the cigarette. He hears the glass shatter against the floor of the outdoor restaurant as he walks back into his hotel room.

Maurice closes the balcony doors, their windows heavily taped, behind him. With his back pressed against the doors, he surveys the room, one of the better rooms, in one of the better hotels in town. It has been his home for almost two years. A mirror is propped by the doors, zigzagged with the same black tape. There is a rectangle of wall, less grimy than the rest, above the bed, where the mirror would have hung. The bed itself, a less than generous double, occupies most of the room. Behind the bed, a fireplace of a headboard, and at either side of the headboard, a reading lamp masquerading as a candle. Opposite the bed, there is a fridge, and a small plastic dustbin. There is a Formica desk against the wall, a framed picture of Elvis Presley, squint, hanging above it. A small bucket chair, upholstered in mauve fabric with a floral print, keeps its own company in the corner. Everything is clean, or as clean as can be and there is a sharp citrus smell in the room. He has scrubbed, wiped, polished and scoured every surface of every item of furniture, even the underside of the desk and the stubby wooden legs of the bed. It has been his home, and now he has to leave.

There are few possessions. A meagre stack of bottled water in the corner, some cans of dog food beside them; the latter a hurried and mistaken purchase as the troops drew near. These he will leave for the cleaners, or the next unfortunate occupant of Room 1213. A tan suit, so crumpled as to be tessellated, lies across the bed with arms spread-eagled, ready for the morning: a matching fedora laid on the pillow. There is an ashtray on the table, empty, and beside it a British passport. While the passport may not be genuine, it is the result of precise handiwork. The photograph at the back is recognisably our man, although it is far from recent. The grubby vanity of an ageing man, Maurice thinks, holding the book open in his hand. He checks the holdall under the bed, and amongst a rummage of clothes, dinars, dollars and pounds tied in small bundles, there are six more passports with as many different names. He will not be checked at the airport: that arrangement has already been made.

The bedroom is satisfactory, Maurice decides, and he walks into the bathroom. Mangled electronics lie in the tub, green fragments of circuit-board veined with gold, shards of imitation chrome casing, splinters of dark plastic shell, all smeared with dark ink, the same ink speckled across the shower curtain. He smashed and battered, crushed and pulverised his laptop with a hammer a few hours ago. Not orthodox, not procedure at all, but Maurice was keen that neither side should see the data stored on the machine, see the shabby structure around which his work had been flung. These remains he will ask Callaghan to dispose of. That seems the most prudent option. Callaghan, his only friend left in Baghdad.

On the toilet sits the head of a shredding machine, the power cable trailing through to a socket in the bedroom. Beside the latrine, a large pile of paperwork has been stacked, the last task before breakfast. Maurice sits down, cross-legged on the tiled floor, positioned in front of the toilet bowl. There is no other option: he had thought about using the wastepaper basket as a brazier and burning the papers, but this would have set off the fire alarm. Or the suspicions of guests on any neighbouring balconies.

He fans out the paperwork across the bathroom floor: plans and maps, photographs and negatives, expense forms and receipts, and a ream of his own reports back to London, all nonsense. Not just his own: everyone had it wrong. Lousy judgement built on bad fieldwork, bad fieldwork built on misguided assumptions, a Tower of Babel now crashing down around them all; still eagerly read by his customers, who themselves had built lousy judgements on bad promises, built bad promises on misguided faith. It had started out with such promise, Maurice establishing a network of stringers through the city and out in the regions. A web with Maurice at the centre, feeling the machinations of his foes by touch like a spider. But lies, lies, all of it.

He viewed the pages with numb alienation, as people do when seeing a common word in front of them on a page, struggling to comprehend the strange combination of its letters. Many of the documents had been defaced in pen or crayon. 'History comes around twice, first tragedy then farce' is scrawled at the bottom of a faxed page of mug-shots. Smiling stickmen have been drawn at the bottom of a recent report home: they are dancing around a fire. 'Exterminate all the brutes' is scratched in red pen across a photocopied diagram of a missile. Many pages have simply been mutilated with a sharp blade. He should have left this line of business, left of his own volition rather than being recalled, tried to start afresh somewhere else. Men like him start out with the best intentions, but that is – not enough. Maurice starts the shredder and begins to feed the bundle into the teeth of the machine, two by two by two, flushing every time that the bowl fills up with ribbons of paper, streams of data long since corrupted.

Finished, he gets up, his legs slightly numb. He walks into the bedroom, now bright with sunlight, and out onto the balcony. There are now cars in the streets, people walking towards the mosque. The day's smog has already started to form, pressed between the city's buildings like a morning mist. He lights a cigarette and leans against the railing. So he would be another man, in another city, perhaps a better man. Perhaps, perhaps. That was up to someone else, it would depend where they would locate him next. In the distance, on the other side of the river somewhere out beyond the Green Zone, he can hear the hotplate crackle of gunfire. His final morning at the Hotel Palestine, his final morning in Baghdad: he decides to go downstairs for breakfast.

In the early days, before the invasion, Maurice had enjoyed being roomed at the Palestine. It was the quiet of the storm, at the very centre of the sandstorm of events shrieking around it; like Casablanca in the movies he liked to think. There was a camaraderie between the men in his line of business, the unilaterals, the staff and even the secret police.

Maurice had watched *CNN*, over in the al-Rashid hotel, the night that Bush had delivered his ultimatum to Saddam Hussein, and when they returned to the Palestine, they found flags from across the world, beach towels, sheets with messages scrawled in English and in Arabic, hanging from the balconies of the hotel, all there to greet the coalition when they arrived. He flew a Union Jack from his balcony that night, and he has put out the same flag today to mark his leaving.

Once the assault on the city began, Maurice was disorientated by the speed of events: he could not contact any of his stringers, and not even Callaghan knew what was happening. He had dashed between his bedroom and his balcony, between his television and the conflict outside. State television was the only channel that he could receive in his hotel room at the Palestine: he watched Mohammed Said al-Sahaf broadcasting from the roof of the hotel. 'Baghdad is safe: the battle is still going on,' al-Sahaf fulminated, American tanks visible in the background. 'The infidels are committing suicide by the hundreds on the gates of Baghdad. Don't believe those liars!'

Later, the American tanks fired on the Hotel Palestine, shells exploding into the side of the hotel only a couple of flights above his room. They had not seen the flags, nor the banners that they had left out, nor the television cameras pointing from most balcony windows. A sniper was directing fire on the Americans from the roof, it was said. It hadn't been a snap decision: the unit had phoned command for further instructions, waiting ten minutes before being ordered to fire on the hotel. In the afternoon, Maurice watched as Chalabi's goons pulled down the statue of Saddam in the square. It was hardly spontaneous, but was still almost spoiled, an American soldier momentarily wrapping the flag of Texas around the dictator's face as they tried to drag the effigy to the ground.

American units were positioned around the hotel. Soldiers and APCs, checkpoints and concrete barriers, this was the nucleus of what would become the Green Zone. Maurice was advised not to leave the immediate vicinity, orders straight from London. There were, it was said, disturbances in the street. Watching *Fox* in the al-Rashid, he saw a press conference with Donald Rumsfeld, who was asked about the alleged looting. 'Stuff happens,' he replied, 'television is merely running the same footage of the same man stealing a vase over and over.' He heard that two of his stringers had been found, mutilated and dismembered, in cloth bags out by the Zawra Park. Stuff happens.

Enough – that was some time ago, and many things have changed since. Few men in Maurice's line of business now remain, most of the journalists have gone. The secret police disappeared overnight. Every day, over breakfast, he has surveyed the old guard who remain, nodding cursory welcomes and farewells. The hotel becomes more of a corporate conference centre every day, loud oilmen complaining daily about the quality of the food; construction workers quiet at their tables after drinking it up in the hotel bar the previous night; entrepreneurs, cheapjacks, hustlers and hawkers, these were the people with whom Maurice shared his breakfast table. Gauntlet Projects had taken over an entire floor of the hotel, their Ghurkhas in the lobby and at the entrances to their floor, sub-machine guns chambered and ready. This morning, a conversation with an Australian called Sobi, who specialises in what he calls adult entertainment. 'I've been looking round this place,' he advised Maurice over tea, 'and I've checked the scene at the Conference Centre: I think that there's a market here, classy, though, respectful.'

Having checked out, he slings his bag over his shoulder, walks through the marbled lobby and out into the sunlight. Callaghan is waiting in the car park, perching like a Buddha on the bonnet of his Humvee. 'I thought you weren't going to make it,' he grunts, throwing a flak jacket and then a helmet towards Maurice. Callaghan works as an analyst for DoD now, but he used to run field ops. He is lean, wiry and probably wired. He makes Maurice nervous, even though they are friends, especially with his eyes, pupils as small as pinhole cameras.

'It's awfully kind of you to take me to the airport,' Maurice apologises as he climbs into the back seat.

'Hey, it's no big deal. We were going out to Burger King anyway,' Callaghan replies, winking in his rear view mirror.

The Humvee pulls out of the car park, another following behind it in convoy. Maurice looks out the window, scales of sunlight glinting across his eyelashes as he squints at the hotel behind him, looking up to see his balcony for the last time. He finds his balcony but the flag has gone: perhaps the cleaners have taken it away. The vehicle is waved through the checkpoint, a soldier watching Maurice from the roadside. The trooper can barely be twenty. On the other side of the checkpoint, pressed against the concrete ramparts, there is a queue of locals. They watch anxiously as the Humvee departs: Maurice heard that five died at this checkpoint last week, collateral damage, caught up in another attempted assassination, a suicide bomber careening his car into the waiting traffic before exploding.

'It's getting worse, you know,' Maurice ventures.

'Course it is,' Callaghan retorts, 'these sand-niggers don't know how to run a bazaar, never mind a country. The sooner that we're out of here the better.'

'Stuff happens, you know.'

'Oh yeah, I know,' Callaghan shouts, thumping his chest, turning round in his seat to face Maurice, 'I so envy you, man.'

'Keep your eyes on the road,' begs Maurice and the

conversation ends. They had got clear, onto the airport road now, and Maurice could feel the acceleration of the Humvee as they sped on towards Baghdad International. This was the part of the journey which he never liked, the part which was known to most as RPG Alley. He felt as secure as he could, Callaghan driving after all, whose general strategy appeared to be to keep his foot on the accelerator, fishtailing between lanes to increase the difficulty of a clean shot. 'Don't worry, buddy,' the American hollers, 'there's enough extra armour bolted to this thing to withstand a nuclear bomb!'

The squat minaret of the control tower becomes visible on the horizon and soon they have arrived. Callaghan goes to find Burger King while Maurice checks in, and returns with burgers and sodas for both of them. The burgers are packaged in small red boxes, 'Have it your way' printed across the top. 'The best meal in town,' Callaghan ventures, burping once to punctuate the point.

The flight to Amman is called, and the men hug awkwardly. Maurice says that he will keep in contact, but he knows that he is lying. He is waved through security, Mr Maurice Chapman, and on to the boarding gate. There are dozens of people waiting for the flight, a popular route now that it is too dangerous to drive to Jordan anymore. While waiting, he watches planes taking off and landing: he sees a huge transport plane, a C-130 coming in to land, skidding sideways through the sky as it descends, firing flares underneath it, bright magnesium tips burning through the sky, leaving furrows of ash in their wake.

He boards his own aeroplane, a Royal Jordanian FW-4000. The plane taxis into position but is delayed at the end of the runway, ready for take-off. Maurice looks at the dozens of people around him, Jews, Muslims, Christians and probably even the atheists and agnostics like himself, lined up in their aisles, heads bowed, praying for mercy. And then the plane lurches forward and into the air, engine roaring, banking left and right over the airport as it continues its steep ascent. Maurice watches as the helicopters on the runway below become smaller and smaller, until they are nothing more than spiders in the desert, watches as the city disappears behind him.

As the plane levels, and the cabin becomes quiet, Maurice feels calm. He sighs, knowing that tomorrow he will be a new man in a new town. Perhaps even a better man. Yes, the world is in order again. He closes his eyes and falls asleep.

Outside Broadcast

THOMAS BRACKENBURY

I opened my eyes. I couldn't move. God was sitting on the end of my bed, visible in the half light from the street, because I always sleep with the curtains open. God said, 'Hello, you're awake.'

I knew immediately what was happening: I'm not stupid. Sleep paralysis. For the unlettered among you, sleep paralysis is what happens when your brain tries to run two programmes at once when you are asleep. The result is that you awaken, completely unable to move a muscle, while what you were dreaming manifests itself in front of you. Sometimes you can snap out of it, and move, with a supreme effort of will, but usually you drift back down to the lower levels thinking, *I should have done something about that.* It has happened to me enough times for me not to be terrified; just scared. God's lips didn't move with speech; neither did mine. I said, 'Hello' back.

I hope that I smiled. I knew that it was God, but I hadn't expected God to be a slightly overweight naked woman in her thirties, with thick, wavy red hair. Specifically, a favourite model of woman. God smiled. She said, 'I read your little paper. I was impressed.'

'Which one?'

'The one about me.'

'I haven't written one about you recently.'

'Don't be defensive: I'm not angry. It was your paper on the *soul*; you can't write about the soul without bringing me in somewhere.'

'I suppose not.'

'I've always enjoyed your papers.'

'Good. I'm pleased. I know that you are a dream: can I move, or go back to sleep now?'

'Every girl likes being called a dream, I suppose.' She shifted her weight, and I felt the bed move. I made a concentrated mental effort to move a hand. It didn't work. She added, 'I particularly enjoyed the ones where you went way off track. I know that I am supposed to be *unknowable* in the true sense, but it's particularly entertaining when you make a bigger hash of it than normal.'

'Thanks.'

'Don't mensh. It's cool. Do you remember that piece you wrote a couple of years ago? About the technical difficulty of having sexual congress with an angel?'

'I might do . . .'

'*Have* you ever had an angel?'

'They were *all* angels,' I told her.

God grinned a big grin, and leaned forward to wag an elegant finger in my face, 'Nice one,' she said. 'Nice one.' Her breasts swung as she moved. God is love. Who am I to argue? 'Your current thesis is that the life force in sentient beings, that has been identified at last by Puthoff and his fellow Americans, is the same thing as the soul.'

'Yes, that's where I started. My zero point.'

'I don't know why it took them so long; I've been giving them enough clues.'

'You leave them in very odd places. No-one expects to find a new piece of evidence concerning the existence of the Holy Spirit in a thirty-year-old black-and-white Western film.'

'Oh. You noticed that, did you? You saw *The Man Who Shot Liberty Vallance?*'

'Yes, but if you had wanted the chosen ones at MIT to pick up on it sooner, you could have concealed it in plainer sight.'

'I sometimes have a bit of a laugh with you lot.'

'I realised that. It was my first step to wisdom.'

'You could have fooled me.'

This time I made a supreme effort. It is like wrenching your consciousness back into your body, and bringing your body back under control. If you can move any part of your body the dream packs in, and returns to Neverland. Nothing moved, except God again. She shifted a little nearer to me, and said, with a dead radio comedian's voice, 'Stop messing about.' Then in her own voice, which I will admit is breathy and attractive, 'Tell me the rest of your theory. I want to know how you got there.'

'I went to a lecture by an astronomess named Heather Cooper. Nice girl.'

'Yes, I think so too.'

'She explained how an unknown planet can be discovered by calculating back from a wobble observed in the orbit of one we already knew about. I knew that there was no organ in the body bearing a label *here sits the soul*, but I wondered if we could instead conclude the soul by observing its effect on something else.'

'Neat.'

'I think so, too.' God and I smiled at each other. Exchanging mild witticisms with the Creator of the Universe was a new experience for me. 'So, once the Americans had identified beyond the shadow of a doubt that there is a life force in living things, my thesis began to write itself. The life force that Puthoff and others describe conforms, depressingly, in most respects with what religious teachers have been telling us about the soul for 5,000 years.'

'Longer.'

'I'll take your word for it.' I remembered to try to move again, but couldn't. I was still wood from the neck down. 'So if the life force is the soul, does it have an observable effect that can be consistently demonstrated?'

'And you found, of course, that it did?'

'It's pretty obvious, isn't it. When the soul is present, a body is alive and functioning. It's vital, in the sense you always intended. Once the soul has jumped ship, you're just so much compost. I can't think of a more observable effect than that, can you?'

'No. That was always going to be a problem.'

'You agree with me then? It's official? Man has a soul, and so do lots of other things?'

'Yes. Of course I do. It's very logical. You solved the problem.'

'What problem?'

'The one posed by that irritating radio fellow who called it the *Meaning of Life, the Universe and Everything* and then killed himself trying to answer it. His brain blew up.'

'I'm sorry about that.'

'So was I. He told some very good jokes, and gave me a walk-on part – like you. You realise that it's the, *so do lots of other things* that will cause trouble, don't you?'

'I'm glad you noticed that as well. Once you get to the point of believing that Man has a soul, you have to ask yourself the question, is it logical that *I* have a soul but that a fish, for example, hasn't?'

'. . . and you did ask, of course?'

'Yes. It's *not* logical. If I have a soul, then so, most likely, has the fish – on a smaller scale, if you forgive the pun.'

'I thought that you'd get that. Albert warned me.'

'This is where the position really opens up, and starts to ask and answer its own questions: for instance, why does my soul require a more complex and sophisticated machine to inhabit than the fish's?'

'I could argue with you about the *sophisticated* sometimes, the average thirty year-old makes me shudder . . . but I see what you mean. *Why*, then?'

'Because, in its turn, my soul is more complex and sophisticated than the fish's: it has more complex and sophisticated needs. I think that means that a soul grows and develops just like biological bodies develop, but not on the same timescale. The essential difference between my soul and that of the fish's, is that my soul is the elder, that's all.'

'. . . and?'

'As soon as the fish's soul has fulfilled its development potential for that particular body and brain it will jump ship, and the fish will die.'

'And its soul?'

'Will grab another fish, if it still needs to do fish, or hop into something slightly more complex and interesting. Say a hamster.'

'A hamster.'

'What?'

God gave me the Mona Lisa smile,

'I was just making fun of you. I have a wicked sense of humour. Do you fancy a shag?'

'No. Discussing my work with you is scary enough. Anyway, wouldn't that be, well, blasphemous – even to *think* about?'

'I don't see why. Mankind has been shafting me for years: why should you be any different?' Deep sigh. 'OK. Give me the rest of it. You're telling me that the logical probability is that Man has a soul, and that it trans-migrates: reincarnation.'

'Yes, I'm afraid so. The Pope is going to be very unhappy.'

'Get to the crunch: the punch-line. What *is* a soul?'

'It's a parasite, isn't it? It has a symbiotic relationship with its body – they need each other, after all – but the bottom line is that it's a parasite; located somewhere in the nervous system. Additionally it's likely to be a paranoid schizophrenic parasite, because it doesn't know that it's a parasite until it makes the jump each time.'

'*Makes the jump?*'

'Leaves one body for dead, and finds another. Do please try to keep up.'

'Oh, I will, I will . . . and I was hoping that you might – that was a bad pun, by the way; I'm really into puns.'

God shifted again until she was astride me; the duvet between us. I felt her weight on me, pinning me down. Despite myself, I tried to move a part of my body. It wasn't a hand this time. But, I've already told you, in dream paralysis *nothing* works. All of God's hair is dark red, chestnut, and she doesn't shave under her arms. Perhaps God has been French all this time. She has a great line in deep, sad sighs. She asked,

'. . . and that's it?'

'More or less.'

'. . . and you won't change your mind about the other thing?'

'Not unless it's a dying man's last wish.' Chat-up lines you could have died for. I tried to grin my *you're gagging for me* grin. That didn't work either. God smiled. It was the smile of every woman in the World. She said, 'I erased your paper, of course, after I read it.'

'What?'

'I wish that you wouldn't keep saying that. I'll find you some-one with a wider vocabulary next time round. If you need a next time, that is.'

'Why, then. *Why?*'

'Because no-one's supposed to know yet. Just our little secret.'

'*Our?*'

'You, me and Albert. He knew all along, but he kept it to himself.'

'I wouldn't.'

'I know.'

A long pause. I know why God appears to be a woman. It's because even if you look at a woman's face a million times, you can still never tell what she's thinking. It was the first time I had dreamed of talking to God. I should have had a thousand crucial questions for her, but I couldn't think of one. I felt lazy. I felt myself drifting down away from wakefulness. Back to sleep. I wasn't going to be able to snap myself out of it this time. That was a pity, because I probably wouldn't remember the dream on waking. Then my attention was captured by a strangely little popping sound that almost appeared to come from within my body. Very gentle sounds. Bubbles in champagne. Three of them. I asked, 'What was that?'

'Heart attack,' God said.

The Beast

EWAN GAULT

Ah don't know how long it hud been lyin there, silent or greetin. Oor strimmers were on before we went intae the garden. It felt like returnin tae the scene of a crime; the charred rags of a sofa hangin limply round rusting springs, a TV that never worked smashed on the patio, the crunch of broken glass. A flat multicoloured kids ball lay at the edge o the path. Iggy booted it against the wall o the hoose. It hit like a slap in the face.

Steve started muttering 'scum, cleaning up aftir fuckin vermin.' His head which grew out of his shoulders as if some wean had drawn it on and forgotten the neck wis red raw. On the juicy sides of his purple lips sizzled bits of spit. He started to cut away the overgrown grass with long vengeful sweeps. Ah fixed the gut on ma machine an followed. The grass wisnae as damp as ah expected and didnae git tangled in the head o the machine. A couple ay bits o glass pinged against ma shins bit a wisnae really payin attention. Ah mind takin off ma goggles and starin at the hooses windaes, a blank reflection of the sullen sky. Wan o the panes hud been broken, a jagged hole totally black. Ah hud a daft notion that if you put your ear to that hole it wid be like listening to a seashell.

'Fuck, fuck sake, fuck.' Steve had unclipped his strimmer an jumped back as though stung. Iggy turned round with a smirk but it died on his face. On the ground was a cot or top part of a pram. It had blue corduroy material round the outside and looked new and clean. Inside amongst the frilly lace and stuff wis a babies face. There wis sumthin wrang wi it like it wisnae quite real.

'Is it, you know,' Iggy faltered. Ah crouched down on the ground remembering a time on holiday being dared tae touch a beached jellyfish. Ah felt it with the outside of ma finger. It wis cold but smooth.

'Get an ambulance,' ah said touching the baby's cheek, asking whoever you ask in these moments that it be brought back tae life.

'Do you think we'll get the rest ay the day off pal?' Iggy asked, rolly cupped under hand, eyes creepin up and doon ma left trouser leg.

'Ah doubt it.'

'Tight cunts,' he hissed, 'ah could go mental in the heid fae a shock like that.'

'Too true,' ah agreed.

Steve wis flappin around the polis. 'Well ah surmise that the poor girl must hae been in some state to do that.' Steve always used the word surmise when talking to suits. He wis shaking his head showing his human side. Poor Steve it said havin to do a shitey job like this and put up with bobo grafters like us. He caught me watching him and snapped, 'Have neither of youse got ma strimmer oot ay that gairden?'

Iggy wis suddenly busy picking a sticker aff the vans dashboard and there wis nowt in the paper so ah went. The gairden hud a grand view o the hills. Pale and bald they looked today. Since comin here ah hud promised maself that ah'd take a walk along their tops, look down at the grey lonely towns holding all these people together. Only ah knew ah'd niver bother. Ah picked up Steve's strimmer and started headin for the van when ah noticed that someone had carved letters into the door. They looked newly done, sharp and edgy. 'The Beast' it read.

At piece time the next morning we listened to the local news on the vans radio: 'Police are keen to know the whereabouts of the mother of a four-week-old baby found by workmen in the Burnside Estate. Reports from hospital describe the baby's condition as poorly but stable. Serious concern for the welfare of the baby's mother have prompted the police to appeal for her to contact them as soon as possible.'

'Did ye hear that, fuckin mentioned on the radio.'

'Naw as if they said yir names.'

'That bairn, wid, hae, been, deid, if it wisnae fir us,' Iggy jabbed his fingers and words intae the air. 'Yir jist jealous cos you wis aff skiving.'

'Ah dinnae care,' mumbled Frank.

'And where were you yesterday, summit to do wi that cut on your head?'

'Aye that wis the missus,' said Frank wi a lazy smile, 'came roond looking fir money and ended up beltin me wi her brolly.'

'Could, hae, had, yir, eye oot, pal.'

'Ken, flung her doon the stairs like.'

'You didnae tell the office that,' asked Steve.

'Naw, ah jist phoned up Jock and telt him that ah wisnae comin in and he said "how" an a said "cause ah'm sick" and he said "how sick" and ah said "well put it this way Jock ah've jist been shaggin ma ain sister."'

'Right lads.' The van shook with pale laughter before Steve snapped, 'The three o youse better get started or wir naw gonnae finish the route.' Cutting down the Field End wis a piece o pish, jist under trees, roond manhole covers, the bits the 212 could-nae reach. The machines were motorised so all you had tae do wis keep them under control. No wan could speak tae you cause o the noise they made.

Once Steve wis oot ay view we stopped an sat on the warm engines of oor machines gulping juice. Everywan drank Irn Bru, always the 750ml glass bottles. Each teams howff wis full o bottles stored till Christmas when they were banked bringing in hundreds o pounds. Frank and Iggy launched intae intrigues aboot who had been thieving fae whose shed and what percent-age share each contributor should receive. Frank started tellin me enthusiastically that ah wid get at least 10% of the teams share if ah kept goin through ma bottles at this rate.

'Fuckin junkies,' hissed Iggy as a group ay crooked skeletons twitched intae view. The lads aw hated junkies. Jist before ah hud started here Iggy hud gone over a syringe wi his mower and the blades hud fired the needle intae his leg. He wis still waitin fir blood test results.

A lassie wis wi them, hands stuffed in an oversized jacket, face too tight as if someone had grabbed the skin on the back o her heid and pulled. Ah wid niver hae recognised her fae this distance if ah hadnae seen her last week. She looked terrible, worse than ah remembered. Ah thought aboot the places you'd have tae go, things you'd have tae see to look that bad. She wis talking tae wan o the men. Ah mind thinking that he looked like a picture ay this mad wee guy that ah haud seen hangin on a board ootside a pub in Glasgow. The Scream or sumthin it wis called. Well gie that boy a manky white tracksuit an a base-ball cap and that wis whit wis looking at me. Ah kept ma head down. Stupid bitch ah thought, better naw recognise us.

* * *

When work finished ah'd walk intae the town centre tae catch ma bus. Aftir ma first day ah wis faced wi the usual problem as to whin this might arrive. As wi jist aboot every stop in the country the locals hud takin it upon themselves tae vandalise the timetables plastic covering makin it impossible tae read. Ah stood there pondering whither this wis a symptom of the curse ay havin nothing tae do or whither it resulted fae knowin that they werenae goin anywhere so why the fuck should anywan else. Anyways it wis at this moment that she appeared standin there fiddling wi cold hands at her little girls purse.

'It's been a long time,' she said, not looking up, 'are you back?'

'Well ah'm here.'

'Naw, whit ah meant wis huv you come back fir, ah mean did you come back because?'

'What?' She sniffed, looked confused. 'Are you alright?' ah sais. 'You look terrible.'

'Ah'm jist fine,' she answered wi a smile that said ah wid never know. 'But Johnny there's sumthin ah have tae tell you.' She reached her hand out, all knuckles and bones, fingers perched lightly on ma folded arms. It wis strange hearing someone say my name. She looked at ma face wi a mad twinkle in her eyes which both attracted and repelled me. She started tae speak but ah saw ma bus slidin in. Ah wis fucked if ah wis gonnae wait till god knows when fir the next wan.

'Listen Jody ah have tae shoot, that's ma bus.' She sortay looked down as if ah hud hit her in the stomach.

'Well, can we meet tomorrow, here? Ah'll be waiting.'

'Aye, nae bother.' Ah mustered a grin and a wink. It took me ages tae find the correct change and the bus driver wis the typical sour-faced cunt. Like you've got a hard job sitting on yir arse aw day. As we turned ontae the roundabout ah caught a glimpse ay her small and alone, like a heron by a river, hunched up and waiting. Ah sat down and read the words of long forgotten teenage lovers scrawled on the back of the seat in front of me and thought about what ah'd be havin fir ma dinner.

The next day Steve hud us started doon the Field End at twenty to eight. You could tell the wife hud been nippin at him, the way he wis chargin aboot. Iggy hud fiddled wi the wires in his strimmer so that he got an electric shock every time he tried tae start the machine. We stood around looking concerned trying no tae piss ourselves laughin.

After he threw a fit we started cutting; bypassin the occasional soggy mattress, piles of newspapers half burnt by lazy paper boys. Ah wis singin away tae maself whin this big caveman throws his windae open.

'That fuckin machines keeping me awake.'

'Aye it's keeping me awake an aw,' Ah laughed, strolling on. Lunch wis gid wi Steve in a monk telling us thit he wis gonnae take the aftirnoon aff. We felt pretty justified in jist lyin back fir the rest ay the day. Iggy wanted to wrap tinfoil around the vans tracker so that we could go and look at girls comin oot ay the High School.

'As any fitba manager will tell ye, if they're gid enough they're old enough,' he cackled.

'Do you mind if we dinnae do that and jist sit outside Sanne Primary fir a bit.'

'Fuck sake Frank, ah knew you were sick but ah didnae think you were that sick.'

'Naw it's naw that,' said Frank looking strangely embarrassed, 'jist the wee wan started school a few weeks back an ah've naw seen her in her uniform.' We sat outside the school like a squad o right fuckin weirdos. Frank jumped oot when he saw his ex. Ah watched him clumsily running to her, picking at an imaginary scab on his elbow as he spoke. Back in the van he watched the kids bundle their way oot ay school. 'Does she naw look braw in her uniform?' he said, drummin his fingers on the wheel. 'She said she'd get her tae wave.' He hit the horn. 'She said she'd fuckin wave.' He sat back and rolled a fag. 'That's wummin for you all over, they're that bitter and twisted.' He pulled heavily on the fag, eyes screwed tight. Ah noticed fir the first time the long dirty nails on his right hand. 'Dinnae get caught there son,' he growled, 'tear your bloody life apart.'

'No Frank,' ah whispered, 'ah'll try and not.'

Aftir work ah wis walkin tae the bus stop outside the glass works when ah heard a pair o heavy boots clumpin along behind me.

'Yir goin the wrang way pal!' shouted Iggy. 'Mind if ah chum you intae town?'

We fell intae step, Iggy babbling on about plans for the night, which ah seemed to hae become involved in. Across fae the bus stop I spotted Jody, starin oot o café windae, chewin on a paper cup like she'd been sitting there all week. Ah leant against the shelter tappin ma steelies to a tune that wasn't really playin in ma head, looking at the chewin gum constellations and praying that she wouldnae see me. When ah looked up she smiled and gave me a nervous wave. 'Dinnae like yours much,' Iggy chirped, following ma stare.

'What's that?' ah said, pretending ah hadnae been listenin.

'Ah wis jist sayin, you dinnae ken that bird do you?'

Ah thought about sittin on her bed pickin at the boughs of hardened candle wax that grew on the whisky bottles she used as holders. She always smelt slightly of candles, looked even more impressively bored in their light. Slightly stoned eyes, flicking ash nonchalantly on the carpet, a private smile itching her lips as she watched the broken television fizz in the corner. A couple of hundred; what are you thinking, are you okay, am ah annoying youse later.

'Naw, never seen her before.' And the bus trundled by and we were gone.

Fran wis walkin along the road like he hud a boner. 'That's obscene,' ah said as ah walked and he hobbled down intae the Field End. Ah spied Iggy leaning against a lamp-post, hoody pulled over his head.

'You got it?' he asked. Fran nodded. 'Ah know jist the place. Left a few tins there.' We stalked down through the estate tasting the nights air feeling free and dangerous. Aftir a bit we nicked intae a layby near wan o the most derelict blocks.

'Nothin but smackheeds left in that place,' nodded Fran. Iggy crouched behind a grit bin and displayed the beers. I squatted next to him while Frank undid his belt and brought out an airgun.

Iggy looked along the length of the barrel, fag hanging limply from the side o his mouth, smoke curdling the fresh chill air. In the pale orange of the street light his face looked serene, ancient. Ah hud an intense urge tae hug him but at the same time the knowledge that this was the last thing ah wid do. Ah sipped at the cold beer and shivered.

'There's wan o the bastards now.' He hud the scummy clothes, the walk that made him look like he wis jist aboot tae shit himself. Ah watched Iggy's face tighten as he pulled the trigger.

'Hit.' The junkie cursed, threw a punch at an imagined assailant and scuttled off. 'Did you see that?'

'Aye, nice wan.' Ah snickered. Fran inhaled his rolly appreciatively. We sat back and got stuck intae the beers whilst waitin fir the next target. Music wis comin fae wan o the further away flats. Silhouetted revellers danced behind windows. It all seemed so far away, like looking at fish underwater.

'Can ah have another beer?'

'Dinnae need tae ask Johnny, jist dig in,' he flashed me a tobacco-stained grin, his face burnt into my memory by an approaching cars lights.

'Pigs,' hissed Frank. We ducked down below the bin. The lights shone on the tangled brambles and dusty clumps of grass around where we sat. The engine stopped and ah waited for the doors to click open. Fuck getting caught sittin in a bush wi a gun and these two cunts. Ah began tae lift maself so that ah could see over the bin. Ah wis gonnae leg it the moment they moved.

It wis a plain car, a man and wummin sittin in it bletherin. Ah wis aboot tae make a cheeky comment aboot they two shitein themselves when ah saw her face. The bloke wis sayin sumthin but she wis jist lookin oot ay the windae as if he didnae exist. Ah ken that look ah thought. He wis doin all the talking but she jist kept on starin intae the darkness. Finally she turned, looked at him and shrugged. He handed her some money and she unfastened her seat belt. As she leaned towards him ah felt a scream crawl down ma throat. He made his seat go back and her head dipped down ay of sight.

'Is that dirty bitch doing what ah think she's doing?' asked Iggy, his unshaved cheek brushing close to mine. 'Fuck me she is,' he muttered. Ah drank fae ma can, dank taste of flat beer in ma mouth, bile in ma throat. Ah swallowed hard.

'Finished already,' exclaimed Iggy. 'Must be a real pro.' The cars engine started and ah felt a purring in ma stomach as it whirled off intae the night.

'Leaves a bad taste in the mouth,' said Frank wi a twisted smile, 'doesn't it?' Ah smiled back, stood up on legs that felt like they hadnae been used in years.

'Ah huv tae go now,' a voice said and ah wis up and walking, not heeding Iggy's protests. Far up above a flight of geese could be heard clacking their way across the nights sky. Ah looked but couldnae see them in the moons pale light. They moved on, their chatter growing faint.

Ah stood outside the end house on a dead end street. A condemned building that no wan could be bothered knocking down. Metal shutters had been screwed over the windaes tae stop kids breaking in and worse things breaking out; a jagged memory, cry in the dark, a hurt that nobody heard. Ah moved intae the gairden, held ma breath, trying to catch sumthin amidst the nights lonely noises. Close tae the house ah touched the doors damp wood, scratching off flakes o paint wi ma nails. There were scars, cuts running here and there. Ah followed the faint letters they made and remembered. 'The Beast' it had said. It didn't feel as sharp as it looked.

Blinds

JACKIE KAY

The Blind man arrived at nine thirty to measure my windows. I've not long moved in and am up very late most nights adjusting to the new house and its different noises in the night. The boiler is quite different to the old house. And there is a strange loud clunk noise every time the toilet is flushed or the cold tap turned off. Nine thirty felt quite a challenge for me to be up and showered and dressed for the Blind man. I was more than eager to have them measured and made because I am now living in a terraced house and next door can see right into my kitchen. One of the woman next door waves the minute she sees me which I find disconcerting. I lived in a corner house before and never saw anybody from any of the windows.

We all want friendly neighbours of course. But too-friendly neighbours fill us with alarm and dread. I made the Blind man a pot of fresh coffee. Something about him suggested to me that a cup of instant would offend his senses. I still had lots to be getting on with, boxes here and there that needed emptied, a heart that needed sorting, but I thought to myself, what kind of human being are you if you can't make a fresh pot of coffee for a man who has come to give you privacy? I've taken two weeks off work to settle in. It still feels like somebody else's house. It feels like play-acting my life living here.

I measured four heaped spoons from the plastic brown spoon into my brand new cafetière. I found two new white mugs in the new cupboard. I told the man I had chosen different colours for each of my three kitchen windows. 'Very Chorlton,' he said. 'Very trendy.' Then he said, 'Very brave.' This made me feel a little queasy. I had never had the chance to choose everything. I've always lived with extremely assertive people, so I am not quite confident in my tastes. I got the milk out from the fridge even though I guessed he was going to say he liked it black and strong. 'Why should choices about carpet colours and so on worry us so much?' I said. 'I've woken myself up in the night worrying about the colours.' When you think of all the problems in the world and all the things there are to worry about, isn't it horrifying to wake yourself up worrying about the colour of your kitchen blinds, or the floor tiles or the colour you have chosen for the hall carpet?

'These are big choices,' he said. 'Choices are scary. All choices. All decisions. Scary stuff. The amount of people that take ages to make a choice, then we go, we fit the new blinds to their window, whatever kind they like, roller or roman or Venetian, and they scratch their head and stare and then say in such a terrible disappointed voice, oh they don't look like how I thought they'd look. And I say and what did you think they'd look like? And they look back blankly and say, oh I just thought, I don't know, I thought that peach would be richer. Or that plum would be plummier. And the voice trails off, you know. Like it has entered some world where the colour they truly wanted does not actually exist. Oh it's terrible, terrible.'

I nod. Again I can't quite shake the uneasy feeling. How do I know when they come and put up my three different colours, my brique (which nearly put me off, being spelled with a q), my damson and my terracotta that I won't be like the women he describes? 'It must be lovely to be decisive,' I say wistfully. 'Mustn't it? Don't you envy the people that make decisions and stick to them?' He sips his coffee, considering. 'Yes and no,' he says after some time, 'Yes and no.'

I'm not sure whether it is the fact that I am up too early or feeling hung-over or even that I am quite lonely in my new life, but the Blind man's 'Yes and no' sounds to me like rocket science. It sounds the real thing. Who needs Freud or Derrida when the man comes and says yes and no like that and sips his coffee pensively? 'I am a self-made man,' he says to me. 'I have been this successful because I've said no and I've said yes and sometimes I've had to admit my mistakes. I still keep my hand in at the measuring so as I keep in touch with people.' He pats my dog. 'Nice dog,' he says. 'I haven't seen that kind before. What kind is it?' 'It's a Tibetan terrier,' I say. 'My mother says there's something wrong with people that don't like animals. Here's my mother for you.' The Blind man steps out to the middle of my kitchen floor and opens his arms. 'Here's my mother.' He is a man of about fifty-five with dark brown hair and a handsome face, very polished shoes. He's wearing a smart designer suit. 'Here's my mother. All religious people are sexual misfits. All people that don't like children are weirdos. All children that aren't allowed to mix with other children are vessels for their parents. Oh yes.' He closes his arms. His voice has changed while he does his mother. 'She's quite definite you see about everything. There's not a thing she doesn't have an opinion on. She could do with a bit of yes and no.'

I pour him some more coffee. He still hasn't measured my windows, but what the hell. He's been here in my new kitchen for half an hour. 'I've got very confused about everything. I can't decide whether to have the brique colour one on that window or that one,' I say, pointing to the bottom window and the middle one. I notice the woman next door at the sink. She is wearing her glasses and a top I haven't seen her in yet. He says, 'Make sure that the very different colours go next to each other so it looks deliberate. You don't want to look as if you've just run out of colour and gone for the next nearest thing.' 'Oh no! I definitely don't want that!' I say, the alarm rising in my voice. The next door neighbour waves at her window and smiles. I wave and smile back. I can see her looking at the Blind man wondering who I have got in. I've had so many men in the house recently and they all end up in the kitchen with me having a cup of something: the carpet man, the shelf man, the boiler man, the bathroom man, the kitchen man. The carpet man told me all about his marriage problems and liked my choice of carpet colour in the hall so much that he said I should take up interior designing. I slept so well that night – bliss. 'So,' he says, 'I would go for this one on that window, this one on that one and this one on that one.' He sips the fresh mug of strong black coffee. 'My mother has been driving me insane recently. It's not her fault. She is grieving the love of her life who wasn't my father. The last fifteen years of her life she has had with this man. They went out on lots of lovely drives together. And her big problem is what to do with the car – the lovely little car that took them on all those special day trips, to the Lakes, to the Peak district, to Derwent Water, over the Snake pass. She doesn't want to sell it and she doesn't want it sitting in the drive. She's shifted all her grief onto that small red car.' 'Give it to me,' I say, half-joking. 'I could do with a car.' 'It's in beautiful nick. It is MOTed up to its eyeballs.' I imagine lovely bright headlamps. 'The upholstery and the engine, everything is perfect. She'd love you to have it. She would like you, my mother. What is it she says about the Scots? You can trust a Scot before you can trust an English person. She's Irish. So that's sorted. I'll bring you the car when we get the papers back. It's a fair exchange, this is very good fresh coffee. My mother always says trust your instincts about people. But my mother prefers my brother to me even though he never sees her and I'm the one that actually does everything for her.' 'The ones that are the most loving are not the ones that are most appreciated,' I say. 'Exactly,' he says. And I notice his eyes have filled. 'I'm a self-made man,' he says. 'My Blind company is the most successful in the whole of the country. I've worked myself up from nothing. The wife thinks I'm too generous. But my mother says generosity never goes wasted.' He looks out my bottom window. The sky is big outside, big and blue and bright. 'Right,' he says. 'I better get out the measuring tape. Do you want them inside the frame of the window or outside?' 'Inside,' I say decisively. He clambers up onto the kitchen surface and starts measuring the bottom window.

'Actually, I've not long got the dog back,' I say quickly. I don't know why. I just want to tell him because he has been telling me about his mother and because he is giving me a red car. He looks round from measuring the bottom window, the one that looks out onto the corrugated iron shed and the graffiti and the waste ground. He makes a note in his little book. 'Did you have a custody fight over the dog then?' he laughs. 'Yes and no,' I say. 'Did he want to keep the dog then?' 'Yes,' I say and I hesitate and then I say 'She.'

He doesn't miss a beat. 'My mother says a dog chooses its master. The master can't really choose the dog. Did the dog follow you more or her more?' he asks. He is on the second window now. 'Me more – definitely,' I say. For some reason I feel very shy in my kitchen and can't wait for the roller blinds to be fitted and pulled down. 'How long will it take for them to be made?' I ask as if it was a life and death question. 'Two weeks, not more than two weeks. We are very quick. My mother says, if a person is reliable that's all another person wants really at the end of the day.' 'I think I love your mother,' I say. 'I think I'll love her car.'

'That's what she needs, somebody to look after her car and to love her car. You see the car has become him now. And she looks out at it in the drive and she says she just can't bear to see it.'

'I got the dog. She got the car,' I say. 'Well, a dog is better than a car,' he says. 'I'll tell you a story, right,' he says, looking back at me from the third window. 'Are you sure you are getting these right,' I say. 'What if we've been so busy talking about cars and dogs and broken hearts that we get the blinds all wrong?' 'Not possible,' he says. 'Anyhow who said anything about a broken heart?' 'Your mother's heart sounds pretty broken,' I say. I have my hand across my chest. It is quite tight. It must be to do with getting up so early. 'It is. I've never seen grief like it. Grief like that, it's like an animal. She's not eating. She's not sleeping. She's whimpering. She's sluggish. She's not herself. She's not my mother. The least thing and the tears come. And it's me that gets it. I'm the one that's there.'

'I haven't told my mother yet. I've just told her I moved.' The Blind man stares at me. 'Oh really?' he says. 'Well my mother always says do things in your own time. Everybody should live the way they want to. We never know what goes on behind the blinds.' He laughs as if it is his first cheap joke of the day and it has made him frivolous. 'Is that a line you say a lot?' I ask him laughing. 'Well, even Blind men have to have some patter.' He makes for the door. 'I better be off. Lovely coffee, perfect coffee. You'll have a dog and a car and three new brave blinds. What more could you want?'

I smile at him. 'What does your mother have to say about

blinds?' I ask him. 'Oh she hates blinds – especially the Venetian ones; she is a curtains woman. She's for the curtains if she goes on sobbing at this rate.' We shake hands again. Maybe we should shake three times for the three different blinds, I say.

We shake hands heartily. My neighbour appears at her window again and stares in. 'My mother says never trust a weak handshake,' he says and shrugs his shoulders. He must be about fifty-five. On impulse he leans towards me and kisses my cheek. I will be back with the car, he says. I don't believe he will. I don't believe he believes he will either. I wave him goodbye. He opens the door of his black BMW by pressing his key. He takes off, waving. I close my door. It is ten past eleven and what have I done today? I have got my windows measured and showered and made some coffee. Days in the new life can be measured slowly, I say to myself. Now it is time to take the dog for a long walk. I shout Walkies, Walkies. I've noticed I've started talking to the dog out loud more since I've left her. 'Whose Mummy's good dog?' I say. 'Mmm? Who is Mummy's good dog? What is love like?' I say to the dog, 'What is love like?' My neighbour appears at her sink again. I think she must be making soup. Her lover comes behind her and kisses her on the cheek. I get the lead down from its hook. The blinds will arrive in two weeks and then I will be able to shut my eyes.

The Accents of Birds

JOANNA LILLEY

Antonia makes their meals from scratch, grinding onion seeds, crushing fresh coriander, grating ginger root. Her daughter, Cassie, sitting at the kitchen table sculpting plasticine, can smell which curry recipe her mother is following. Cassie, Antonia knows, loves curries. Aged six, she has the palate of a thirty-year-old.

Antonia hears the scrape of Cassie's chair and turns to see her standing up. 'Can I go in the garden, Mummy? Before it gets blue-dark.'

'Just for a few minutes. I'm putting the rice on.'

Cassie loves to run up and down the long garden path and Antonia is careful to keep the shrubs and grass on either side from growing over it.

'You'd never know, would you,' Antonia's mother says each time she visits, standing at the kitchen window watching Cassie run.

Antonia wants to say: 'Put a plant pot in her way on that path and you'd soon bloody know.' But she doesn't. Her mother knows no better and never will. Whenever her mother speaks about Cassie, her voice is a composite of pride, wistfulness and embarrassment. Antonia has got good at listening to voices since she had Cassie. She's learned she can't hide anything from her daughter; Cassie knows exactly when her mother's anger is on the cusp of humour, when her weariness is on the cusp of tears. People who can see don't realise that everyone keeps all their secrets in their voice. To listen best, Antonia has to shut her eyes but she can only do this when she is on the telephone to people, not, of course, face to face.

Antonia goes over to the open window and calls to tell Cassie tea is ready.

'I heard a blackbird, Mummy,' says Cassie as she comes in. 'And some chaffinches.'

As she eats, Cassie says: 'It's still blue-dark, isn't it? It's not black-dark yet. If it's black-dark, does that mean I have to go to bed?'

Cassie recently learnt that the sun sets a minute or two later every day for half the year and then earlier every day for the other half but it's hard for her to understand about stars and planets and satellites. Antonia has tried to explain by clasping Cassie's hands round oranges and apples and calling the orange the sun and the apple the moon. Yet it's difficult to imagine a burning star ninety-three million miles away when you've never seen one.

After she has put Cassie to bed, Antonia turns all the lights off and moves around downstairs in darkness, finding, tidying with her fingers, toes, nose. In the sitting room, she sits on the settee, closing her eyes so that even the street lighting outside is shut out. Tomorrow she will be forced to consider whether they must move. Away from the only house Cassie has ever lived in, away from her clients, and away from her mother. Cassie needs a better school, a special school for special children with special needs. But hasn't the word specific replaced the word special, indicating that her child is not special any more? A specific school for specific children with specific needs. A school that already knows things about Cassie that she will take all her life to learn.

A man called Simon North from the specific school is coming tomorrow. He will assess Cassie and decide whether to offer her a place. The school is forty miles away in Perth. If Cassie attends, they will have to move and Antonia will have to find another house with a long garden path for Cassie to run up and down.

It would be a great relief to find a good school. The teachers at her current school try hard but they don't have time to become experts on Cassie. They say she's artistic – as if this extra gift compensates for the one she failed to receive – and perhaps she'll become a sculptor or a musician. But Antonia doesn't care what Cassie becomes; she only cares what becomes of her.

In the morning, Antonia is surprised when Simon arrives, and cross for being surprised. He is blind. Completely blind, Antonia suspects, not like Cassie. Then again, perhaps how Cassie will become. The doctors are hardly reassuring.

Once the door is closed behind him, Simon reaches out his stick to find a wall, moves over to it to lean his stick against it and begins to shrug off his jacket.

Antonia says suddenly, 'Here, let me take that for you,' and peels the jacket off the arm that has remained in it. 'I'll hang it up here,' she says, 'on these hooks by the door.' She realises she's treating him how she treats Cassie whenever they are somewhere unfamiliar, giving a running commentary, and immediately wearies of hearing her voice. 'Please,' she says, hoping the anger in her voice is not revealed. 'Let me know how I'm supposed to help you, if you want help. I'm only used to dealing with Cassie. At her school, none of the other children have the same disability as her. I don't know anyone else . . .' She stops talking, watching Simon's face.

He's smiling. 'It makes a change,' he's saying, 'to meet someone who's angry with me. Usually, it sounds as if they're on the verge of tears. With sympathy, I suppose, or relief that they're not me. I'm never quite sure which.'

'I'm sorry,' she says. 'I'm not angry with you. I don't even know you. I'm angry because I can't help. I mean I can't really help. I can only do my best.'

She stops talking because she knows that it's not only Cassie who's going to be assessed this morning; she'll be assessed too. Schools don't want difficult parents any more than they want difficult children.

'It's fine,' says Simon, sounding as if he means it. 'Tell you what you could do, though, you could pass me my stick.' He holds out his hand, thumb stretched away from his fingers, and Antonia places the stick gently against his palm. 'So,' he continues. 'Where's Cassie? Sounds as if she's upstairs.'

Antonia takes Simon upstairs to Cassie's room where she's sitting on the floor playing with her dolls, listening to Vivaldi's 'Four Seasons' on a CD player, humming along.

'I'm not hot-housing her,' laughs Antonia. 'She loves all this classical stuff.'

'Hi, Cassie,' says Simon, bending down. 'Vivaldi, eh? Are you a Nigel Kennedy fan or more of a purist?'

'More of a purist,' repeats Cassie, and Simon and Antonia laugh.

Antonia asks Cassie to take Simon to the sitting room while she goes to the kitchen to make them a cup of coffee. She's glad to leave him for a moment. She can't stop looking at his face. How sometimes he closes his eyes as if he doesn't know that sighted people keep their eyes open all the time unless they're asleep. How his eyes are a cloudy, chalky blue behind his tinted glasses, yet his eyebrows and hair are dark and that he's actually very attractive and does he know it? And what she really wants to know is whether he's ever seen or if he's been blind from birth. At what stage in an acquaintance with a blind person can you ask that question, if ever. Do you have to wait for them to tell you?

In the sitting room, Cassie has spread a sheet of newspaper on the carpet and is placing her drawing pad and colouring pens on top of it. 'I'm allowed to draw in here as long as I don't make a mess,' she's explaining.

'I'm ashamed to say it,' says Antonia, putting a tray on the coffee table, 'but I used to get cross when Cassie drew. She'd sit drawing at the kitchen table and keep going over the edge of the paper onto the wood. I suppose I shouldn't tell you things like that. I mean, that I get cross. But, to be honest, now I love those marks all over the table as much as the pictures she does.'

'All parents get cross with their children at some point,' says Simon. He's sitting on the floor beside Cassie. Antonia feels silly sitting above them in an armchair but joining them on the floor would feel silly too. As Simon gets up from the floor and gropes for the settee, she realises, though, how much easier sitting on the floor must be.

'What support do you get?' he says. 'Does Cassie stay on for after-school care?'

'She won't stay,' says Antonia. 'She has tantrums if the other children go home and she's still there.'

'Do you work?'

'I paint portraits, which means I can work from home. I do a lot of pet portraits,' she laughs. 'From photographs that I take.'

'Fantastic,' says Simon.

'But that all stops when I collect Cassie from school. I can't work once she's home. She somehow takes up all my attention.'

'Do you mind if I ask where her father is?'

'He left when Cassie was a baby. When it was obvious she wasn't going to be your average child.'

'Certainly not average,' says Simon.

Antonia nods in agreement but then remembers he can't see her. 'No,' she says. Her voice, because she hasn't been expecting to use it, is hoarse.

Two days later there's a letter from Simon North offering Cassie a place at his school. And within a couple of hours, he telephones and asks to visit again, to tell them more about the school and arrange a visit, he says, and to talk to her about her doubts.

When they hang up, Antonia cannot recall ever mentioning her doubts. Dealing with blind people is, she decides, like dealing with mind-readers. Imagine a whole school of them, super beings with special powers. Did he hear it all in her voice? That she's scared she won't earn enough from portraits in Perth to support Cassie, that she feels guilty about moving away from her widowed mother, and that she's worried about how long it will take Cassie to get to know a new house as well as she knows this one and what that might do to her confidence.

'You don't want Cassie to have the stigma of going to a special school,' says Antonia's mother. She's sitting at Antonia's kitchen table, rubbing at a felt-pen mark with her finger as if that will erase it. 'You want her to learn as much as children do at normal schools. If she's in a special school she'll sit around playing the tambourine and drawing pictures all day.'

Antonia tries to prioritise her indignation. Should she defend her own profession first, or Simon's school which she hasn't seen yet, or Cassie herself?

'Hang on,' she says. 'You're worried about the stigma of going to a special school when your granddaughter can't even see anything more than an inch from her face. She's as good as blind. She's going to need all the help she can get and the crappy little special needs unit she's in now just isn't up to it.' She is about to go into the sitting room to fetch the brochure Simon left them but then thinks why the hell should she. If her mother is interested, then she can ask for it.

'You never know, the doctors might be able to do something.'

'No, Mum. We do know. If anything, Cassie's eyesight is going to deteriorate altogether. There won't be any more cute little blue-dark and black-dark comments, there'll just be dark-dark.' Antonia rushes from the room to get the brochure after all. Any excuse to leave the room so that her mother can't see her tears.

By the time Simon arrives the following day, Antonia no longer has doubts. She has told her mother they are moving and, because her mother won't drive, that she will be happy to pick her up from the railway station any time she wants to visit. And sometimes, of course, because she is her mother and perhaps can't help her views, she will drive back to visit.

When he comes, she lets Simon talk.

'Antonia,' Simon says, pausing.

'Yes?'

'I'm at a disadvantage here obviously because I can't see you, but I'm not sure you're listening to me, are you?'

'Yes. Well, I suppose no. I've already decided Cassie should go to your school.'

'But you haven't seen it yet.'

'True, but, if this doesn't sound too insensitive, maybe seeing isn't everything.'

Simon laughs. It's a deep, long laugh and Antonia can't stop herself giggling and then wonders why she's trying to stop herself.

Her laugh dwindles only when she thinks how can Simon ever be attracted to a woman he can't see. Of course it's not only about looks but, really, how does a relationship with a blind person ever get going? Do you have to be courageous enough to say what your voice may have already revealed? With Cassie, it's easy, they hug each other any time they like.

'Tell me,' says Antonia quickly, to get it over with. 'If you don't mind. Can you tell me something about what it's like for Cassie? And for you, of course. Do you mind?'

'I can't tell you what it's like for Cassie. I had my sight until I was eighteen when I had a car accident. It's different for Cassie because she's had severely impaired sight from birth. She lives in a different world to mine. How can I possibly, for example, know what her dreams are like?'

'I'm sorry. I shouldn't have asked.' There is surely irritation in his voice.

'No. You should have asked. You only want to understand what life is like for Cassie.' He hesitates. 'Faces,' he says, speaking slowly. 'For a while after I lost my sight I remembered faces just as if I was looking at a photograph. But they began to fade and disintegrate. Voices have become the equivalent of faces, in a way.' Simon starts to speak more quickly. 'Sometimes I forget to smile because a smile is generally something shared with, triggered by, another person. Sometimes I close my eyes because there's no need for me to hold them open and my friends think I've fallen asleep when I'm actually paying great attention to them. And you get paranoid. You start to imagine that people you know, friends, are walking past you and not bothering to say hello because they're in a rush or they don't like you any more because you're a drag, and they think you'll never know they were there so what does it matter.'

Simon has stopped and Antonia doesn't reply immediately because she is thinking about what he has said and hoping that Cassie doesn't start forgetting to smile.

'You know what would be a great thing to do? For Cassie, I mean,' he says. 'The next time it's windy or raining, wrap her up and take her outside. Get her to listen to all the different sounds. She'll know this but rain falling on grass sounds different from rain falling on stone. And the wind tells you how tall trees are, how big buildings are. Wind and rain make a two-dimensional world become three-dimensional.'

'We'll both do it. My senses need developing too. Perhaps not my sixth sense, though.' She looks at her watch. 'It's time to collect Cassie.' She looks at him but his face is directed at the window, not at her. 'Why don't you come with me? Cassie would love that.'

'That would be great. You'd need to give me a hand, though. I'll hitch a ride on your elbow.'

Coming back from school, the pavement is wide enough for Cassie to walk in between Simon and Antonia, holding both their hands.

'That's a blackbird,' says Cassie as they walk by trees. 'There are some great tits and a blue tit. I think.'

'We started learning together from tapes, but her ears already have a much bigger vocabulary than mine,' says Antonia.

'Mummy says we're moving to Perth, Simon,' says Cassie. 'Is that where you live?'

'Yes, Cassie, it is.'

'Do birds in Perth have a different accent from the ones here?'

'I don't know, Cassie,' smiles Simon. 'I think that's for you to tell us.'

Pandora

LYNDA McDONALD

She was a child given to silences. Not because she didn't understand or didn't care. She was just overwhelmed by a family that had so much to say. When she ventured her first sounds, they improvised verbal scenarios for her. When she took her first step, their exclamations made her aware of her audacity. With a whoosh of air through her padding, she plopped back to earth.

To be helpful, her sea uncle created the talking doll. He carved it with paring knife, awl and tiny-toothed hand plane. Shavings from its dainty face lay curled on the floor, the grain of the wood undulating like contour lines that mapped out an endless smile. The doll's cheek bones were pronounced and angular; her lips, curvaceous, pouty, oaken, hard.

The body was a mermaid's, decorously covered in circles of lace. She had tiny seed pearls round her neck. The child's mother made the tail with a piece of material from her workbox. The box had been her own mother's – a time-darkened wicker treasure trove of buttons, arcane sewing implements and slithers of fabric that represented the entire married and maternal lives of both women. Each remnant had perfectly matched thread on a homely wooden bobbin.

The tail material shimmered. It was once a party dress. But this body with its jaunty fin lay limp. The doll's face was enigmatic. Its hair was the first cutting of the child's own hair. A wavy blonde swag. The eyes were green glass chippings. The child was five years old and she hugged the doll, which was destined to speak, as best she could.

You call it Pandora he told her – for she might have become a box. She might have become a table or a drawer, like the rest of the tree, then a shelf, and so on and so on until so little was left it finally became matchsticks.

The fist-sized shape that became Pandora had been drift-wood riding the spume. It was caught in the net. He heard its commotion as it tried to break free, upsetting the fish. So he removed it to stop it tearing the nets to let the fish escape. It was determined.

One day, the doll seemed to have tears in its eyes. Resin, he said. Resin seeps. That's all. And he laughed his booming laugh at the thought of it crying real salt tears. His laugh filled the house until the child thought she heard the blue and white china tinkling on the dresser. See, and he wiped away the tears with a man-sized tissue. Held it out to show the tears were peat-coloured, not clear. On the tissue, the moisture spread into bigger pools. The child knew it was tears. She hugged the doll that would talk for her, and smelled wrack and mussel shells and vinegar. This was her talking doll, but she must teach it first.

A gottle o geer, her uncle said through sealed, but moving lips, wrenching the little curtain ring inside the doll so its mouth opened angrily. She doesn't understand, said the child.

Ber ber bla shee ha you any woo? His sealed lips jigged. Is that better? She could taste the doll's displeasure at having nonsense words put into its mouth.

She opened the doll's mouth gently with her finger the first time. She breathed warm breath into it. When it was time for her uncle to go away, she stood with the doll on the doorstep to wave him off. She wanted the doll to say safe trip as her mother did, but it either couldn't, or wouldn't, make the words sound right.

Keep practising. I'll teach it a sea song when it can speak

properly, he called back: and his laugh made the birds rise up in a cloud. He went out on the tide at first light. Later, the doll's mouth clacked emptily when the child pressed down the ring.

The mermaid doll was allowed to go to school on the child's first ever school morning.

'Don't let the doll tell the teacher your name,' her mother said. 'You must tell the teacher yourself.'

'Anne,' answered the doll at register time.

They were asked to talk about their special things:

the rabbit called Bob
a tent for sleeping out on the drying green – in the daytime
a watch to show the time when I'm under water . . . when
I'm not afraid of water anymore . . . when I can tell the time
the dressing up box so I can be a cowgirloranurseoragypsy

'My mermaid,' said Anne. When held up to show them, the mermaid doll looked sulky, until her mouth was opened and Anne made her speak.

See see see sea sea Sea.

The doll's head turned defiantly left and right, snap snap, in its single plane, to challenge anyone to say the words better. But she had taken the words from the children and no one could speak, only stare; and covet a doll that talked all by itself.

'Make her say things,' they said later, crowding round. 'Make her say *my* name.'

When Anne was eight, she told them that Pandora had decided not to speak anymore. She would listen. Her school friends could speak to Pandora and she would take in their words. She would not tell. They could give Pandora their secrets and she would guard them. She would protect their secrets for a sweetie. They could tell her things for their play piece. They might whisper for a chocolate bar.

Pandora is on a diet now said Anne some time later. They could now tell Pandora for ten pence. So Pandora collected their secrets. And, as Anne had been an observer from an early age, she understood the importance of order. She wrote out a little docket with the person's name on it. Eventually Pandora established a sliding scale of charges based on seriousness.

Occasionally someone tried to buy one back. Encourage Pandora to forget. But that was extra. Forgetting cost an extra twenty pence.

When Anne's arithmetic got better and she understood about shopping, she offered a reduction. Tell three for the price of two. Pandora's services were a bargain.

I stole from the sweetie shop. A liquorice boot lace. (A liquorice bootlace, its scent thick and oily and exotic, snaking along between my teeth, leaving its shadow.)

I've hidden my mummy's ring. She'll think it's my wee sister 'cos she's always taking my things.

Tell Pandora.

I broke a cup and saucer from Nana's best set. I put the pieces in the bin.

Tell Pandora – I'm not listening.

I want to kill my baby brother. I saw how to on the telly.

And later: *I love that boy in P7.*

And Pandora would answer, with increasing clarity as time went on, 'Your secret's safe with me.' (*I shall swim away on the tide and take your secrets with me and leave them on a lonely coral reef* – although she didn't say all that.)

It was a mistake. I love my baby brother now – he smiles at me all the time. He likes me best. And for 20p, Pandora forgot what had been said before. Just like that.

When Anne was ten, the teacher told them the story of Pandora. This Pandora let terrible things out rather than keep them in. Anne, the pragmatic child, was interested in that. It seemed a contradiction. She went home and took Pandora out of her bed. Pandora's bed was an empty fish tank, given to Anne by her oldest brother, for whom girls had taken the place of guppies and angel fish. Pandora had seen him with these girls. He had a special place he took them to, overhung with drooping trees, dark as the seabed Pandora had come from.

Anne sat Pandora on her lap and told her the terrible story of what her namesake had done. (By way of practice, she had Pandora interject her shock at intervals.)

Anne was called from P7 to take Pandora into the classroom of the new intake. Even the shyest would talk to Pandora. There was no chance of charging for their secrets, however, with the P1 teacher and the classroom auxiliary ever vigilant.

Anne saw her dad out with a lady who wasn't her mum. She always thought he looked happy at home in a distant sort of way; but this was different. I don't know how, Anne thought, but he looks younger. How can my dad suddenly look younger? I shall tell Pandora – no one else will listen. But Pandora was not to be found.

I might become a professional ventriloquist Anne said at home some time later when careers had been mentioned at school.

The sea of voices informed her that there was no money in that. Anne said they shouldn't be so sure. Her dad smiled. Her mother was sympathetic. She offered to give Pandora a makeover – if Anne could find her. Anne searched and found Pandora in the garden shed. Her body had a patina of algae and her tail was mildewed. Anne's own baby hair still clung. Out of her mother's basket, in a flourish, came a Mediterranean blue-green swish of silk from a bridesmaid's dress. The firm wooden body and face were rubbed with tissues and Body Shop cleanser, the hair shampooed with chamomile until it glowed again. Her uncle said he would carefully drip olive oil into her mouth to ease the stiff clip.

But the doll wouldn't open her mouth. And Anne was out of practice and couldn't make her speak. Anne's lips would not stay together. Spittle and nonsense came out. The doll's mouth seemed to droop.

Anne found an old bike in the shed. She decided she would cycle along the canal path to find some peace to mentally chart the life of the successful ventriloquist. She saw her Dad walking along with the woman again. They laughed and they kissed. Anne might have been invisible. At home, no one was invisible. Nothing done ever went unnoticed.

I'll make you another doll said her uncle. Think what sort you'd like. Perhaps Pandora's turned stubborn. Maybe she has something she'd rather keep in. If we make her mouth open, something terrible might come out. He laughed at that.

I am no longer considering ventriloquism as a career, Anne announced. Everyone clapped with relief. Her dad was there. He clapped too, joining in as he always had. She realised how little he had ever said over the years. He'd been a listener, like herself. Was this new woman giving him chance to speak? Anne thought of her as a ventriloquist with her dad as a great big soft doll. It didn't make Anne smile. She was suddenly worried about all the things she knew.

Anne took the bike out to the canal again. This time she had the towpath to herself. Pandora was in the saddlebag, mute with displeasure. Anne took her out. Gazed into her sharp green glass eyes. Nothing happened. You know too much she said – and you don't care.

Anne launched Pandora in an over-arm arc into the canal. Pandora landed on her face. Bubbles popped. She flipped over, but the sodden material drooped beneath the surface of the water, tugging down the body with its seed pearl necklace. All that was left on the surface, carried serenely along by the flow, was Pandora's head, green eyes looking forward, lips set, curvaceous, pouty, oaken, hard.

Dear Anne

LESLEY McDOWELL

Sst. Sst. Is all I can hear. Now that she's gone. Coming from the tap in the kitchen downstairs. And thuds outside – footsteps sometimes hard, sometimes soft. I notice them more now. They stop at the front door occasionally. I think they are coming in again. But then there's a cough, the striking of a match, a murmur of voices, clicks that grow quieter as they move further away. And bricks falling, just once. Clumsy, banging against walls; fragile, dislodged by the air.

Everything else inside the house is still. As it has been since yesterday afternoon. Sunlight elbows through a partly pulled curtain, a rule broken with the first screams. I'm in its way; it warms me. All those months with the curtains closed, I'd forgotten what the sun felt like. Comfort. Or a plan for the future. A near future, not one years and years ahead, just a few months. That will do.

Dear Kitty
'Little bundle of contradictions.' That's how I ended my last letter and that's how I'm going to begin this one. 'A little bundle of contradictions', can you tell me exactly what it is? What does contradiction mean? Like so many words, it can mean two things, contradiction from without and contradiction from within.

It was just another morning, normal as normal can be under the circumstances. The single alarm clock going off; high-pitched squeaking from beds, floorboards creaking low. Chairs scraping across wooden floors, bed-frames yawning as they're folded up and put away. A succession of visitors padding barefoot to the lavatory (sometimes necessity means a rush back across floorboards to the pot under the bed and a long, relieved pssshhh to follow). Collisions on the landing and cross words over who uses the lavatory first.

Just what happens every morning, when too many people live in too small a space together. All of us, in hiding. It's been this way for two years. And I wait, as I have done every day since we came here, shut away until the noise stops and I am needed.

It is a great thing to be needed. I am more important to her than anybody, I think.

I am her best friend. An ideal best friend. Never complaining if she forgets about me for a few days. Never insisting that I know best, as her mother does all the time. Never making her feel guilty the way Margot does, for being more attractive and clever than she is. A complicit best friend, I admit. I've never said when I thought she was wrong or badly behaved. Or at least, I've never said it openly. I've left it to her to be the judge – she could look over her own words as often as she liked, or as seldom as she liked, and think on them if she wanted to.

The first is the ordinary 'not giving in easily, always knowing best, getting in the last word', all the unpleasant qualities for which I'm renowned. The second nobody knows about, that's my own secret.

It happened just after lunch. Cracked dishes cleared away for evening, raised voices in the kitchen. The usual arguments over dinner and the size of portions. Who had taken too many potatoes at lunch (because it was always Peter and why shouldn't he, he's a growing boy after all). Who would have less that night as a result (Anne doesn't like potatoes anyway and she's small, she doesn't need so much, you can't deprive Peter, he needs a man's meal). Women's voices, not caring who heard. Hoping, maybe, to be heard. And given some support.

But, as usual, no response. The men were all downstairs – Peter, Mr van Daan, Mr Dussel, Otto. The radio crackled, hissed, spat to hit the spot. The men shushed each other for the foreign voices, as familiar now as their own. More crackling and hissing. Then the foreign voices smudged out altogether. But not before enough had been said. The men ran back upstairs with good news and the women in the kitchen forgot about potatoes and equal portions.

And then there was quiet, as always. The August sun warming our dark little tombs through closed curtains. It was too stuffy to stay awake. I might have guessed she would fall asleep like the rest. Even Otto lay on his bed, just for a minute, of course, then he'd get up and finish his book.

I waited, for the time of day we had all to ourselves.

But it never came. I was still shut away when Mrs van Daan's screams woke everyone up. Why she was downstairs at the bookcase I don't know. Maybe she heard something. Maybe she was looking for that ribbon she said Margot had borrowed and never given back. Maybe she couldn't sleep and was taking the usual exercise, up and down the stairs in her bare feet, quiet so as not to wake anyone.

I had never heard screams like that before. Not proper screaming. High-pitched, panicky, pointless. Then breaking wood and orders in a language we hadn't heard in this house. Heavy boots and a groan as a body fell, feet stumbling, pitched against a wall. The boots hit the stairs, punished them with angry beats. The first level – chairs and tables crashed on to wooden floors.

The boots carried on. More stairs – the second level. I heard too many voices pleading all at the same time and then the thick whip of something hard on flesh. More cries, more furniture knocked and kicked and cursed. More boots.

But I couldn't hear her. I wondered if she was there or if she had managed to hide. Not that it would matter – every corner was abused. Beds pulled out, stripped and shaken; books slapped off their shelves; pots and pans yanked to the ground.

That was when I realised they might come for me.

I am her best friend. If they wanted her, they would want me too.

And then I heard her, a quiet warning to Margot who was crying and couldn't stop. And then the curtain was torn down, and the desk tipped over. And then I thought: now, this is when they will find me. This is when they will destroy me.

I've already told you that I have, as it were, a dual personality. One half embodies my exuberant cheerfulness, making fun of everything, my high-spiritedness, and above all, the way I take everything lightly. This includes not taking offence at a flirtation, a kiss, an embrace, a dirty joke. This side is usually lying in wait and pushes away the other, which is much better, deeper and purer. You must realise that no-one knows Anne's better side and that's why most people find me so insufferable.

But they didn't. They left me on the floor in the middle of a pile of old papers. They didn't even look at me – I was just another piece of rubbish. Not at all what they wanted. They had that now.

There's a scurrying sound over my head. The rats in the attic are back now that Mouschi is gone too. The patter on the boards frightens me more than the silence. I'm scared they'll nibble at me if they come down and see me lying on the floor like this. Her film posters are on the floor beside me too. Ripped from the walls and torn up. It could only have been done for spite. They must have known the posters didn't hide anything.

Everything still smells of potatoes. And now I can hear children outside. Their clogs clack on the road. Then – begging in whines, scratching in the rubble. Like the cats and dogs no-one feeds anymore. I think I know she will not come back. She won't carry on from Tuesday. That's the last time I'll hear her.

I am her best friend. And she is – what?

Not what she is to her mother, who has to compete with her for Otto's affections, who sees in her youngest daughter mostly just a cold, ungrateful girl who makes her cry because she wants her father to say good-night to her and who turns her head away the one and only time her mother comes in instead, who makes it impossible for a mother to love her own child and there is nothing in the world worse than that.

Not what she is to Margot, plain, quiet Margot with her glasses and her dead eyes, her frumpy hair and dull clothes who sees a frivolous little sister who shouldn't be given so much attention, especially not by Peter, even if Anne did find Peter first and Margot didn't want him anyway, although she would have liked a friend of her own, especially as she was the older of the two and, of course, she should have had first refusal of any boy in the house.

Not what she is to Mrs Van Daan, who looks at greying hair in the mirror that she can't colour anymore and the wrinkles she can't smoothe over with night cream because she used the last of that months ago and they won't get anymore until the war is over, who looks at Anne and thinks she is the worst example of what happens when a young girl is indulged too much, because Peter, her precious boy, will surely be trapped by that conniving little minx if the war lasts much longer and they never get out of this dreadful annexe.

Not what she is to Mr Dussel, who has to share a room with her and thinks she is as irritating a girl as all girls are, but even more so because she has an unjustly inflated opinion of herself and has actually had the temerity to argue with him over who has the greater right to the room for privacy, when he has important work to do and she only has some silly girl's scribblings to put in her diary.

Not what she is to Peter, who was surprised one day to find this girl he'd always thought of as a nuisance, just Margot's little sister, asking him to explain himself, talking to him about how he felt and why he felt it, when he'd been used to keeping everything to himself and who believed he preferred it this way until she dragged it all out of him and made him put it all into words.

And not what she is to her father – a gift. It is the only word he can use for a bright, mercurial girl with shiny black hair and a wide smile and eyes that look straight at you, who can make everyone laugh even when boots march past outside and planes moan overhead and bombs hit houses just a few streets away and there isn't anything he can do to stop it.

You can't imagine how often I've tried to push this Anne away, to cripple her, to hide her, because after all, she's only half of what's called Anne: but it doesn't work and I know too why it doesn't work.

Too many Annes in this cramped space, I think. Lots of public Annes. But only one private one. A private Anne that only I, Kitty, am privileged to know. She calls me Kitty as though I am a separate being, distinct from her. As though paper and ink are muscle and nerve and bone. As though pressing a dark nib against my white pages, jabbing marks across my skin, makes me into a body, complete and perfect on my own. As though that body, now created, isn't just a reflection of hers. As though I have a life of my own.

Because I don't, of course – for that I would need a voice of my own and no diary has one of those. She could make me a body but she could only give me her own voice, and I must echo her day after day, page after page. I won't be heard anywhere. No-one will hear what Kitty has to say.

Sometimes, if I really compel the good Anne to take the stage for a quarter of an hour, she simply shrivels up as soon as she has to speak, and lets Anne number one take over.

Footsteps again. Stopping outside. I wait for them to move on but they don't. I hear scuffling behind the bookcase downstairs. Then the door breaks and I know what that means. They are back.

But no. I am wrong. Only one person comes in. A man is sighing as though this mess in front of him was created just to annoy him. And yet there's another tone in the sigh. Something else – sympathy, when he thought he had no sympathy left. I hear his knees crack as he bends down to the papers on the floor behind the bookcase. There is no point in his reading them, or trying to smoothe them over, to see if they might be important. It is better for him to get this over with, as quickly as possible, he knows that. They won't be coming back to collect anything.

He has brought a brush with him, I hear it soft against the floor. He begins to sweep up, broken china, paper, bits of wood, all caught up together as they never would be if everything wasn't broken. He will use the makeshift mop they left behind, just some rags tied on to the end of a wooden pole that used to hold up clothes on a line of rope in the garden outside. And muttering as he comes up the stairs, slowly. An old man. Only an old man would mount stairs slowly. A young man would bound up them, the way Peter used to every evening because he'd been indoors all day and walking up and down wasn't enough exercise for a boy with all his energy.

I wonder if he'll notice me when he gets to this room. I am hidden partly by newspapers, but he will feel something hard and heavy if he tries to lift them out of the way. Then what will he do with me?

Therefore the nice Anne is never present in company, has not appeared one single time so far, but almost always dominates when . . .

No, I will stop her here. I will shut out this entry, close off her voice. Her voice can only be heard at the expense of mine. No-one hears me, because all they can hear is Anne.

And yet, I am Anne. I am Kitty, to whom she wrote almost every day and because of that, I am Anne too. I am a mirror and an echo, that is true. I echo her words, I reflect her back at herself.

I know exactly how I'd like to be, how I am too . . . inside. But, alas, I'm only like that for myself.

I can't stop it . . . how can I, when I am Anne, when I am Kitty? When we are both the same.

And perhaps that's why, no, I'm sure.

But we are not the same. No reflection is so similar, no echo so exact. No work reflects the body with absolute truth. There is a fault in every copy, and in that fault is where you will find me.

I am not Anne.

I am Kitty. I am the warp in the mirror, the dip in the echo. I am there in the hat that is not quite as straight in the reflection as she thinks it is. I am the weak point in the chin that is not so well-defined as people say. I am the blackness in her eyes that are darker than any photograph can show. I am the sentence that she thinks so beautiful but lasts just that little bit too long. I am the question that she believes she asked only once, but in fact it is there again and again and again.

And if this old man does not pick me up, if he leaves me here among the newspapers and the torn film posters

It's the reason why I say

If he does not see me and take me away with him.

I've got a happy nature within and why other people think I've got a happy nature without.

I won't survive. She will not come back and I will be left here and no-one will hear her and if no-one hears her then I will not be heard

I am guided

His feet crush the papers.

by the pure Anne within

He bends down. A hand touches me.

but outside I'm nothing

The Martha Day Affair

NICOLAS McGREGOR

I leave my office with two slugs inside me. One from the battered hip-flask the late Martha Day used to carry: bourbon, body temperature; the other, a .38 scraping my collar-bone: another souvenir from the Martha Day affair. I keep it there to remind me that all dames, even old dames, are as dangerous as Original Sin. As if I need reminding. I got a lip-glossed high-heeled angel watching over my shoulder with one flashing eye, watching my back with the other.

Closing the door to my office don't stop her watching neither. Sure, the frosted glass with the legend *Frank Irons, Private Investigator* stencilled in white like the chalk outline of a side-walk homicide might hide the details of my face and form from her. Sure, I left her polishing those stiletto-sharp ruby reds she calls nails with an emery strip on the other side of that glass, the kind of dark-haired doll you could take home to meet your mother of a Sunday evening, and rob the bank with first thing Monday morning. But she's watching over me nevertheless.

'Can you remember the first time you saw one of your parents fall over?'

What kinda question's that to ask a man in his late forties? Especially a man in his late forties who carries a heater holstered in his armpit. I try not to take it personal.

'Sure. I remember.'

'Which parent was it you saw fall over?'

'My mother.' Hell, I may have seen my father fall over a dozen times in the course of this dark business I call life. For all I know, I may have even helped him along the way a time or two. There's a nice thought for a rainy Tuesday. The schmuck ran out on my mother when I was two. I wouldn't know him from Adam. I wouldn't mind bumping into him some quiet evening. Wouldn't mind catching up a bit. What's the classic biblical killing again? My mother (rest her soul) used to take my fourth grade Sunday school class, and I seem to remember that it's the jawbone of an ass. Well, if I ever catch up with my ass of a father, he'll get the old Irons one-two in the jawbone alright. Don't know if I'll be able to stop it there neither.

'How did that make you feel?'

'A little nervous . . . amused maybe.' She wasn't indestructible, my mother. I'd known this all my life. But seeing her fall. *Jeez.* Nuthin' prepares you for that. She seemed to fall forever. Like a tree.

'Amused? Interesting.'

'Naw, it ain't nuthin' like that. She wasn't hurt. Just tripped against the sideboard is all. Hell, I've done as much myself.'

'Did you laugh out loud? When she fell?'

'Naw, she might've taken it personal.'

'And what about you, Mr Irons. When you trip against the sideboard, if someone laughs, do *you* take it personal?'

It's been known. Remember Orlando? Orlando the Fix, finger in every pie, exceptin' the cherry kind? Man, he shoulda known better, that time down Dante's. Slid clean offa my stool; what I get for trying to share it with my good friend Mr Jack Daniels. Still, he shouldn'ta laughed, shoulda known to keep his mouth clamped as tight as his boyfriend's tush. Me and Mr Jack Daniels, we go way back. Neither of us look kindly on that kinda behaviour. The Germans have a name for it: *Schadenfreude.* Dante told me that. It means gloating, with malicious delight.

Well, neither me nor Mr Jack Daniels speaks Kraut. We replied in good old American. The meaning's grievous, with bodily harm. When Dante pulled me back – there's few men I'll suffer to get all hands-on with me, but Dante the Kraut's among them – it'd be a while before Orlando would be fixed enough to finger any pie.

Damn it, I'm smiling at the memory. And the Doc here don't miss a trick.

'Mr Irons? *Do* you take it personal?'

'It's been known,' I allow. But the Doc's read me wrong here. If I took things personal, I'd be breaking him up with the furniture right now. Asking a man about his mother falling! *Jeez.*

This is my third visit here. Gotta say, I'm a little less belligerent than before, a little less suspicious. See, I'm used to being on the other side of the desk so to speak: The shrink's desk is over by the window. We're seated in comfortable padded chairs opposite each other in the centre of the room, knees just short of touching. I'm a detective, and I'm used to being on the case, not being the case myself.

Still, I'm coming to respect this sideburned quack. Bald patch the size of a saucer, weak-chinned, normally the kinda guy I despise on sight. Not his fault, but he looks a little like a two-bit hustler out of Carson City by the name of Whistler. Whistler was a squealer, on the payroll of every jelly-bellied trooper this side of the State line, not to mention that of yours truly. If it was going up, going down or just plain gone, Whistler was the man to talk to. Few shed tears when he turned up face down in a Tecoma back alley with a .38 between the weepers. The Martha Day affair again.

So I took an instant dislike to the Doc from the moment I met him. Even the sign on his door got my back up. *Doctor*

Devlin Rush, M.Phil., Ph.D. Devlin Rush. I wanted that name. That was a name that said: *don't spook this guy. Don't even breathe wrong around* Devlin Rush. Devlin Rush *is the kinda guy who'll chew you a whole new personality if you spook him.*

Not that I'd thought Frank Irons was so bad. Resolving the Reservation racket back in the day, I'd hooked up with Melassa Opens-Mouth, that bookish Lakota-Sioux squaw with the perfectly hairless body. Man, she didn't even have down on her arms. She used to sit in bed, reading aloud, running that straight razor of hers here, there and everywhere. That's what I call waxin' lyrical. Remember how she extended her people's gratitude by living up to her name? According to her I'd earned it by living up to mine.

'Frank Irons,' she'd said, her blade hissing slowly down one thigh. 'You know the literal etymology of your name?'

I thought etymology was nine letters across for 'insect studies'. But then, I never was *Times* crossword material. Never advanced beyond the front page and the funnies. So I just shrugged an eyebrow, lit up a cheroot and let her get on with the pillow talk while I admired the view.

'I interpret Frank Irons as *Outspoken Guns*,' she said. Damn me if that wasn't the prettiest compliment I'd ever been paid. *Outspoken Guns. How about that?* 'We Sioux place much faith in given names.'

Blessed be if she didn't back up her claim by putting her own to immediate, energetic and very welcome use.

But ever since the Martha Day affair, I've been on the lookout for a new name.

'Frank *Irons*? Frankie *Irons*! Does all your own dry-cleaning, does you, Mr Irons? Once we're done, it'll take more than a spell at the steamers to sort *you* out.'

Doesn't take much to deflate a man. The weakest barb might not even prick the skin, but when you back it up with a .38, it pierces right to the heart. If I didn't have a lip-glossed high-heeled angel watching over my shoulder with one flashing eye, and watching my back with the other, that's exactly where Martha would've pierced. As it was, she reduced me from Opens-Mouth's avenger *Frank Irons* to plain ol' Frank Irons, a two-bit shoulder-shot gumshoe who needed the services of a drycleaner *pronto Tonto* on account of a) crapping himself and b) not being able to clean his own pants, having just been shot in the shoulder.

So I'd been toying with wiping the slate clean, starting fresh, symbolically purging the memory of Martha Day by changing my name. *Martha Day, you say? Not me. That was some other guy. Some two-bit shoulder-shot Private Eye by the name of Frankie Irons. Me? Hell, no. I'm . . .* who? I couldn't decide. Something classy. Something dynamic. Something I could live with. I read the telephone directory back-to-back. Twice. The people of this town don't do classy, they don't do dynamic. They do Brady, Colin and Jamie; they do Brody, Collins and Jamieson. They do not do Devlin Rush. Maybe all the good names are ex-direc-tory. *Devlin Rush, Private Investigator.* I'd like to know what Melassa Opens-Mouth and her insect studies made of that.

When he opened the door that first time and I discovered that this Devlin Rush resembled a dwarf informer who'd shared one too many secrets rather than the Dolphins line-backer I'd pictured him to be, you might say I was disappointed. I'd thought to come face-to-face with a man's man, a six-foot-six ex-sergeant who'd demand, 'Call me Doc! Everybody does,' (except family, who called him Rush, and close friends, who called him *The* Rush). When the ipso-facto Doctor Devlin Rush ushered me into his office and insisted I call him 'Devlin', I wasn't particularly surprised.

'And if you hadn't been there to hear her fall, would she still have made a noise?'

'What you say?' My mind's wandering. Takes me a second to come back to the present. The Doc's still talkin' about my mother. I try not to take that personal, but a man shouldn't talk about another man's mother when that other man's preoccupied. I'm betting my feelings don't show on my face, but the Doc picks up the vibe. I can see that on *his* face. Give him credit: he doesn't shy back.

'Just a joke, Mr Irons. *If a tree falls in the forest . . .*'

'Hell yeah she'da made a noise.' I allow a bit of the old Irons iron to creep into my voice. 'She weren't no buttercup, my mother. No buttercup.'

The Doc actually leans forward. Guess the old Irons iron's a little rusty. Or the Doc's got absolutely no sense of self-preservation. I admire that in a man. 'No. Buttercup . . . Interesting.' He leans back again. 'How *would* you describe her, Mr Irons?'

'A falling tree, Doc –'

'– Devlin.'

'– Doc. My mom was like a big old falling tree.'

Only, at the end, there hadn't been anyone there to hear her fall, least of all me. Wonder why she didn't use the gun I gave her on the coked-up street-beast who beat her to bloody pulp. About the same time Mom died, Martha Day was putting a slug in my shoulder instead of in my heart, her aim out on account of half her head disappearing. Unlike my mother, I got a lip-glossed high-heeled angel watching over my shoulder with one flashing eye, watching my back with the other.

I tried to track down my mother's killer, but Frank Irons of the Outspoken Guns wasn't home. There was just plain ol' shoulder-shot me. Right when I needed my skills most, they deserted like my schmuck of a father. The streets dried up on my approach. Those contacts I did find all told me the same: nobody knew nuthin'. And I got my usual assist from the cops: they knew nuthin' neither. Now, normally, I'da pushed. Nobody *ever* knew nuthin' until I pushed. But it was the way it was said. Not *nobody knows nuthin'* and *God help me Mr Irons, they'll kill me if I tell*, but *Frankie, sorry, man. Nobody knows nuthin', But if there's anything I can do . . .*

Even Johnnie Solitaire. I tore Johnnie's dance studio apart with my bare hands when he held out on me during the Carson Freight mess. You remember that? He's screaming the entire time, '*I don't know, I don't know!*' but once I dangled his boyfriend from that big old balcony of his, Johnnie spilled the way virgin jailbait don't. So when I turned up at Johnnie Solitaire's pad in the middle of the night, I expected him to sing out, loud and clear. Fear has a way of doing that to a man. Sympathy I didn't expect.

'*Jesus, Frankie*,' (Not Mr Irons. Mr Irons was long gone.) '*Jesus, Frankie, I heard. I'm so sorry.*'

So I spent the hours between sunset and sunup weeping into the pyjama top of a fag dance instructor who knew nuthin' except how to console a broken man. Johnnie Solitaire got me through the death of my mother. I don't need no shrink to get me through that hell again.

'Why do you think you're here, Mr Irons?' the Doc asks.

I'm not here about my mother. I'm here because I want my P.I. licence back. I can hardly come straight out and say that, though. So I tune into Radio Irons, pump the volume way high and broadcast the subliminal half-truths the amateur calls lying.

'Well, Dr Devlin Rush,' (M.Phil., Ph.D), 'my heart's a stone. The stone has a name. The name of the stone is MOTHER. The stone is planted in the Our Lady of Light Episcopal Church cemetery on Fourth and Pentonville.'

Not bad, I thought. Six months since I boxed my dear old Mom; just after the Martha Day affair. I'd stood there, in the rain, my right arm in a sling, my left arm occupied by the crutch. Throwing a handful of the greasy clay that passes for earth down Pentonville way onto the lid of my dear-departed's coffin was the most difficult act I've ever performed. If it hadn't been for the spiritual support of Father Forbes and the moral support of my good friend Mr Jack Daniels, I doubt I'da made it through the service. My lip-glossed high-heeled angel was there, some-where, when I planted the stone. I didn't see her, but she was there: one flashing eye watching over my shoulder, the other watching my back.

I reckoned Dr Devlin Rush accepts I got sent up for six months of mourning. I reckoned he'd think I got three of those months off for good behaviour, and then I was back on the streets, sentence served, but disorientated by feelings of loss and guilt, culminating in deep depression. Far as I could tell, I haven't given him anything else to work with. I thought, *I've a hell of a poker face. Devlin's gotta figure me for playing the Suicide King.*

That was when Doctor Devlin struck me down with the old brick-wall stare. Those slate-coloured eyes, as attentive and unwavering as a double-barrelled Remington room-sweeper, pinned me to my seat. *You're wasted being a shrink*, I thought to myself. *You should've been a Private Dick. Or a fourth grade teacher.* Unblinking, he waited for me to break, to tremble, to sweat. But I *am* a Private Dick, and I've *met* fourth grade teach-ers: I recognise the tools of my trade when they're turned on me. I take a slug from my hip-flask, protocol and Doctor's orders be damned. I'm just psyching up to brick-wall back when he leans forward and puts a hand on my knee. I nearly fall out my seat. There's few men I'll suffer to get all hands-on with me. I decide Dr Devlin Rush is among them.

'I've done some investigating, Mr Irons.' I can't take my eyes off his hand. The back of his fingers are real hairy, like I imagine the hands of my father. 'You know Martha was your mother's name?'

Now, what kinda question is that to ask a man who planted a stone named MARTHA all of half a year ago? I can't answer him, though. I'm distracted by the little circle of red light that's appeared on the back of Devlin's right hand.

'And you're aware that Day was your mother's maiden name?' Devlin's fishin' to make eye contact, but I'm not biting today. I'm looking through the triangular gap formed by his bent body and the angle of his left arm. The window is to his back. The little circle of red light slides up his wrist, briefly disappears only to reappear on his shirt beneath his armpit before vanishing once more.

'Your hip-flask . . . that was your mother's, wasn't it? It has her initials on it.'

I ain't listening. I'm frozen in place looking over Devlin's shoulder at the building across the street.

'Did you kill your mother, Frank?'

I ain't listening. Devlin's got a lip-glossed high-heeled angel watching over his shoulder with one flashing eye, watching his back with the other; the one that's pressed against the telescopic sight of a Winchester M70.

'Did you, Frank? You can trust me –'

There's a sharp report, real Pulitzer Prize material, and blood blossoms on the front of Devlin's shirt. His grip tightens on my kneecap, his lips purse over above his glass jaw, his eyes brick-wall permanently.

My gun is out and in my hand and I slam my back against the wall. I let a few minutes pass before peeking out across the rooftops. Pointless. She's gone, but watching still. Watching over me.

Strange the window hasn't shattered. I have to hit the glass twice with a bronze paper-weight from Devlin's desk before it fractures, and once more before the window caves out in jagged splinters to fall into the street below in a deadly rain. I've cut myself, and there's blood on my hands. The paper-weight is shaped into a bust. I think it's supposed to be Freud. We'd have seen eye-to-eye, me and Freud. I love my mother.

She watches over me.

The Wedding Ring

BERNARD MacLAVERTY

On a morning in June 1904, Annie Walsh, a stout woman in her
early sixties, stood at the ironing board smoothing a white pillow
slip. She liked to use two irons so that she could work continu-
ously – smoothing with one while the other was heating. Her sister
Susan, younger by twelve years, sat on a stool by the kitchen range
with a hanky in her hand. She had not cried for some time, but
it was at the ready because she knew she would cry again soon.

'Will you be needing the goffering iron?' she asked.

'Aye – a wee touch.'

Susan put the poker between the bars into the red heart of
the fire.

'One more iron should finish it,' said Annie. The ironing board
creaked as she put her full weight on the material. Susan readied
the next iron and Annie picked it up. She spat the tiniest of spits
onto its surface, testing it. The moisture fizzed and danced on the
black shine, then disappeared. Annie finished the pillow case and
started on the nightgown. When she came to the lace at the neck
she nodded for the poker. Susan tried to withdraw it from the fire
but the handle was hot, even through the handkerchief. Annie
made a noise with her tongue and grabbed it. It was glowing and
when dust motes touched it they momentarily sparked white. She
quickly inserted it into the hollow tube of the goffering iron, then
grasped the moist lace in her hands and pressed it over the tube.
There was a smell of smoke. The material made sighing noises
here and there as she worked her way around it. When she was
finished she held her work at arms' length.

'Ready?' Her sister sat, not saying anything. 'I could still send for help. But I feel it's something we should do ourselves.'

Annie always wore a gold cross pinned horizontally to the dark material at her throat. If she wore it the right way up the top irritated the underside of her double chin. And she was forever looking down – at her prayer book or her embroidery. Even on other people. She was taller than most and bigger in girth. Mr McDonald, the boarder who had stayed with them longest, described her as 'a ship in full sail'.

'Some soap.' Susan lifted a bar of carbolic from the wall cupboard and sawed a slice off it.

'Is that enough?'

'Remember to wash that knife – or it'll taste the bread.' Annie picked up the pillow slip and ran her hand over its surface. 'The Belfast linen looks so rich.' You could see by her eyes that she had been crying too. But she had finished and was determined not to start again.

Susan thought her sister the strongest person she knew. Everything she did, she did with determination. The knock at the door at all hours of the day and night would be for her – to bring somebody into the world or to lay somebody out. And there were times the two things happened together. Their younger sister, Elizabeth Tierney, had died giving birth to her first child, Ellie. Five years later Ellie's father had died of consumption and the two of them had reared the child as if she was one of their own. All this as well as running a boarding house for three, sometimes four gentlemen.

Annie made a pile of the sheets and pillow cases and set the soap and facecloth on top of the nightgown. Her white apron was stiffened with starch and it created small noises in the silence as she moved about her business.

Susan washed the bread knife then filled the ewer from the steaming kettle and set it in the basin. She looked distraught.

'Be brave, Susan,' said Annie. 'It's all about appearances – giving the right impression.'

'I can hardly believe we're sisters,' said Susan.

Annie picked up her paraphernalia and began climbing the narrow staircase. Susan followed her to the return room with the ewer and basin.

The blind was down, darkening the bedroom. Susan refused to look at the bed and set the ewer and basin on the marble-topped dresser. She stood facing the wall on the edge of tears again. Annie raised the blind. The light was harsh.

'Maybe keep it down,' said Susan. 'I know nobody can see in but . . .' Annie thought, then shrugged and pulled the blind halfway down.

'I usher them into the world and wash them on their way out,' she said.

The figure in the bed was covered by a pink satin eiderdown, which Annie herself had quilted and sewn. She took a breath and pulled it back.

The girl's body lay straight and to attention. A pillow supported her chin and coins weighed her eyes. Annie took them off and the lids remained closed. There was a chink as she dropped the pennies into her apron pocket. The bedclothes fell quietly to the floor. Susan put both hands to her mouth and began crying and repeating over and over 'Ellie – oh wee Ellie.'

'God rest her.'

'I thought she was improving last night,' said Susan, 'when she got up for a while. Said it eased the pain – sitting on her hot water bottle – God love her.'

'And when she was anointed – that helped,' said Annie. 'It was more than good of Father Logan to come out so late.'

'The doctors said there was nothing they could do.'

'That kidney man from the Mater is supposed to be the best in the world,' said Annie. 'It's amazing what they can cure nowadays. Help me lift her.'

'Where's the best place for my hands?' Annie showed her. Ellie was cold to the touch. The two women raised the body and Annie pulled the nightdress off over Ellie's head and down the stiffening arms. They carefully laid her flat again. Susan looked shyly away from the body's whiteness and triangle of dark hair. Annie modestly covered it with a small linen towel. The material remained tented like cloth drying on a hedge.

Then Annie noticed a chain – a long chain around Ellie's neck. There was a ring on it. 'What's this?'

'I dunno.'

'A gold ring. Why would anybody want to wear the likes of that. Instead of on her finger. Down her bosom?'

'I've no idea.'

'A wedding ring too.'

Annie moved to the washstand and poured some hot water into the basin. She wetted and soaped a facecloth and began washing Ellie's face, damping and pushing back the black hair from her forehead, making sure the eyes stayed closed. When she had finished the face she moved onto the body. Susan watched mesmerised by the way the skin moved, just as it would in life. The chain with the ring was in the way and Annie disentangled it and took it off over Ellie's head.

'You've never seen this before?' Annie wrinkled up her blunt nose and held up the chain.

'No. It's just a ring – all girls love to have rings.'

'But a wedding ring?'

'Especially a wedding ring.'

'Ellie could never have afforded this. You know how much one of these costs?'

Susan shook her head. No, she didn't. Sadly.

Annie was about to hang it on the bedpost when she paused.

'There's writing here. Inside. I can't make it out. Susan, away and get me my specs.'

Susan left the room and creaked down the stairs. There was still a faint smell of smoke in the air. It was only recently that she'd needed glasses herself. Before that her eyesight had been good but now, definitely, she needed them for close work like darning or for reading a newspaper. Annie, despite being so much older, claimed she'd no use for them. 'Good light is all you need,' she said. On the rare occasion she did need to see fine print she'd resort to a lorgnette which she kept in the drawer of the bureau bookcase. Susan, now with the lorgnette in her hand, climbed the staircase slowly as if it was the highest and longest staircase in the world. She knew what was coming and was filled with dread. Susan passed the lorgnette to her sister. Annie brought it to her nose and focused on the inscription. 'For Ellie – my love – and – I can't make out whether that's "life" or "wife".' She moved closer to the window and held it lower to catch the light coming beneath the blind. 'What do you think?' She passed the ring to Susan who read it off almost without looking.

'For Ellie – my love and life.'

'In the name of God . . .' Annie stared at Susan – perplexed. Susan handed the ring and its chain back. Annie hung it on the bedpost again.

'What's going on here?'

'How should I know?'

'Who would have given that to her – and her only twenty? Susan, why aren't you looking at me?' Susan raised her head and looked at her sister. 'You haven't been able to meet my eye since we came up here. What's wrong with you?'

'My wee niece has just died.'

'There's something else. I know you of old, Susan. You think I don't know when I'm not being told the whole story?'

Susan's eyes went down again and she began to weep with her whole face. Eyes, mouth, chin, the wings of her nose. She did not wipe away the tears or knuckle her eyes. Annie continued to wash the body, looking up at her sister occasionally to see if she had stopped crying. Eventually she did. Annie unfolded the white freshly ironed nightdress.

'Let's get this poor girl respectable again.' Susan helped Annie insert their niece into it.

'That nightie was a favourite of hers,' said Susan, 'with the wee ruff of lace.'

'She had a rosary of her own, didn't she?' said Annie.

It was kept in the drawer at the bedside. Susan produced a purse. In it – dark knotty beads – and Annie bound Ellie's dead and waxy hands in an attitude of prayer.

'What I want to know is,' Annie looked up, straight at Susan, 'if Ellie couldn't afford a solid gold ring, then who on earth bought it for her? And put such writing in it?'

Annie lifted the chain and ring from the bedpost. She spilled it from one hand to the other with a little metallic hiss. She continued to stare straight at Susan. Eventually Susan said, 'How would I know who bought it for her?'

'All the times you were out together – she never gave you the slightest hint?'

'No.' Susan shook her head. 'Did she give *you* the slightest hint when *you* were together?'

'No. But as you say – we're very different. Ellie was *your* pet. She would confide more in you than in me.'

'I don't know,' Susan wept. 'She got days off. How do I know where she went – or who she went with?'

'So she *did* go with somebody? Who? If you were to guess, Susan, who would you guess?'

Still Annie spilled the chain from hand to hand. Susan stared down at the pink satin eiderdown on the floor.

'You are not going to like this,' she said. 'But I would guess – Mr Burns. I know you despise him but . . . she was very fond of him.'

'I might have known,' Annie almost spat the words out. 'The one and only lodger I ever had to put out. I couldn't stand to be under the same roof one more night after that display of behaviour.'

'It was only a kiss.'

'She had her eyes closed. And for all I know, so had he.'

'It wasn't like that.'

'So you know what it was like. How, might I ask?'

'They were very fond of each other. Maybe, more than fond.' Susan returned her sister's stare with something approaching defiance. 'You know how we take it week about to go to church with Ellie? Weeks she was with me she'd meet up with Frank Burns after mass.'

'Oh, it's Frank now, is it?'

'All three of us would walk in Alexandra Park.'

'So he didn't move away.'

'He's in Kansas Avenue.'

'And you stood by and watched this pair?'

'Yes. But not all the time. I'm sure they met without me being there. Maybe they *were* married – who knows – she talked enough about it – maybe they found a priest who married them. Mr Burns knew a curate in St Patrick's from his own part of the country. There's no give with you, Annie. The girl's dead.'

'Did she ever tell you she was married?'

Susan nodded her head.

'Sort of.'

'And you didn't tell me.' She dropped the chain and the ring onto the linen of the bed and buried her face in her hands 'Susan, you're a fool. An utter and complete fool. Poor Ellie's immortal soul . . . all because of your foolishness.'

'Yesterday – she only told me this yesterday – when she felt so ill she thought she was going to die.'

'She was a good judge of one thing, at least.'

'She said she wished she'd been really married.' Susan shook her head sadly. 'Maybe they weren't married – maybe they only plighted their troth or something – maybe they were only play-ing at being married, playing at being man and wife.'

Annie stared at her sister and shook her head almost in disbelief. She said with some deliberation, 'Susan will you go down and get me a pair of scissors. The wee nail scissors.' Susan stared back at her, then left the bedroom to do as she was bid. She went down the narrow creaking stairway yet again. Annie shouted after her, 'They're in the sewing basket, I think.'

Susan went to the sideboard, crouched and found the pannier where the sewing and embroidery things were kept. She had to scrabble about hunting for the scissors. There was a green pincushion bristling with needles. Tiny hanks of embroidery threads of every colour. Spools of white thread. Eventually at the bottom she saw what she was looking for. She trudged back up to the return room still on the verge of tears. She handed the scissors to Annie.

'She wasn't married. Not truly,' said Annie. There was a change in her voice. It had lost its note of worry.

'How can you be so sure?'

'I checked. Just now. For my own peace of mind.'

'You checked what?'

Annie said nothing but began to clean under Ellie's nails with the point of the tiny scissors. Then she gave her sister a look.

'Jesus Mary and Joseph,' said Susan.

The weather was unseasonable for mid-June. Susan had to hold her hat on her head or the wind would have whipped it, hat-pin and all, as she struggled up the Antrim Road towards Kansas Avenue. In her other hand was the small leather purse Ellie had used for her rosary beads. In it now was the gold ring and its chain – in her mouth, terrible tidings for Frank Burns.

Gorilla Rock

ANNE MORRISON

The first and deepest layer is the most difficult, although caught up as they are in the excitement of building the dam, the girls hardly notice. The water is running fast and cold and stones must be found which are heavy enough not to be washed away. They do this bit quickly, rolling the uneven boulders zig-zag across the rough grass and into the mouth of the top pool, skinny arms numb to the elbows as they reach in and position the stones. Another layer, and the water is forced upwards, spraying out across the bank, soaking their thin socks and synthetic leather sandals. The girls keep searching for stones, carefully placing them on the little wall until the stream is contained. They plug the gaps with small pebbles and easy handfuls of moss that come away from the dense peat with a soft, intimate squeak. The youngest of the girls sits and tickles her face with a bunch of the pale green froth while the others busy themselves, stuffing it into jagged holes in the dam where it turns sodden and dark.

Only a trickle now flows down the breast of rock below. They call this place Gorilla Rock: a wide, near-vertical outcrop surrounded by scrub; a giant sitting upright in the heather, his back set against the hill. At the base of the rock is the gorilla's lap, an oval-shaped pool encircled by smooth flanks of weathered stone. On sunny spring days like this the girls find dry spots and sunbathe on the gorilla's warm chest, lying at peculiar angles, muscles tensed to stop themselves from slipping, jerseys snagging on rough patches as they slide inch by inch towards the shallow pool below. On wet days they do dares: they dare one another to slither across the gorilla without falling or to jump from the far side of his lap onto the glassy chest above. New bruises appear every other day.

The water leaves the oval pool mysteriously, curving over an algae-furred tongue of grey and into a deep crevasse, disappearing altogether for half a mile or so until it comes tumbling out above the shore. Sometimes they use divining sticks to find the hidden flow. Without trying, the girls are surprisingly good at this. They start off blind, closing their eyes and holding the ends of the forked sticks loosely until they feel a subtle but definite tug. Following the line of the gentle pull-pull, eyes half-open now, they take slow deliberate steps until the pointer stick bobs briefly over a particular spot. Lying on the prickly grass, ears to the ground, they hear the gorilla's belly rumbling deep underground.

'He's hungry. I told you he would be.'

'Find food. Find food fast or he'll eat us.'

Today, they will feed him fish.

With the dam secure above them, the four girls begin bailing the oval pool. They use small blue beach buckets and a couple of jam jars, scooping and pouring with wordless absorption. A dark band gradually appears above the muddied water and now the bailing gets difficult: buckets must be laid on their sides and squashed down for the water to be caught and whisked away. The girls are looking for tiny brown trout, fingerlings, quick and furtive as the imagination.

The bailing stops abruptly. The youngest girl has dropped her bucket and is staggering backwards through the pool, her eyes fixed on an aperture the size and shape of a man's fist. The others freeze. All their attention is now focused on the hole.

'What is it?'

'Baby fish?'

The little girl shakes her curly head.

'A big fish then?'

She frowns in confusion.

'Yes. No. Not a fish.'

'Dead or alive?'

She is looking at the hole and nodding fast.

'Alive.'

Like a well-drilled ambush party, the girls creep around the sides of the pool and converge on the hole as one.

'How big?'

'Big.'

'Go back to the caravan and get the white washing bucket.' The youngest wriggles through a crackle of ferns on the downward slope and runs off at full pelt, swerving to avoid gorse bushes and jumping clumsily across ditches. The others watch over the hole and deliberate while they wait for her return.

'Sticks?'

'Sticks might kill it.'

'Bait.'

'What kind of bait?'

Nobody wants to dig up worms; that would take too long. They think about using their fingers, dangling them just below the surface of the water at the entrance to the hole, but decide that the creature is unlikely to be fooled. A rustling behind them, and the youngest child is back, triumphantly carrying a large white bucket. In the end, they decide there is nothing else for it but for one of them to put her hand into the hole and scare the thing out. The second eldest, a freckled, fair-skinned girl with wide, flat cheekbones and a short nose tells the others she will do it.

'The dare to end all dares,' she says solemnly, pulling her sleeve over her fist and clenching the ragged cuff tight in the palm of her hand. 'Just in case.'

'In case what?'

'In case it bites.'

She hesitates only for a second and then pops her hand smartly into the hole. In the same instant, the eel rips out of its hiding place, thrashing and arching with supple, surprising force. They can't see where it begins and ends: it is everywhere in the muddy pool at once, the lithe brown body breaking the surface again and again, the whole length of it whipping across the shallow water. Suddenly the eel seems to collect itself, transforms into a fluid squiggle as definite and elegant as a calligrapher's mark and slips neatly back into its hole. The girls are awestruck. The gorilla and his demanding hunger are forgotten. They want the eel for themselves.

On the second attempt, they are better prepared. Two of them hold the tilted bucket in front of the hole, while the second eldest girl once again performs her feat of ultimate daring. This time, the eel slides smoothly and resignedly into the bottom of the white bucket where it lies twice-coiled and gasping. The girls crouch around the bucket marvelling at the creature's sleek perfection. They run their fingertips along the feathery length of its dorsal fin and let the tiny blunt teeth of its protruding lower jaw close repeatedly on their pink thumbs. They study the rhythmic flickering of the gill fringes and the gradation of colour from deep brown back to pale yellow under-belly. Eventually, they remember that without fresh water the eel will die. They allow him a few inches of clear water drawn from the top pool, enough to breathe in, but too little to aid sudden escape.

And now the girls want to display their daring and their superb prize. Turning their backs on Gorilla Rock, they make for the caravan park. They decide against going first to their mother. She will probably be pegging out washing on the rotary clothes dryer and might have already noticed the absence of the white bucket. Not that that would bother her much. Nothing they say or do ever seems to surprise her. To the girls, she is the living embodiment of benign detachment; her gaze rarely fully focused, her thoughts permanently elsewhere. Sometimes they wonder what kind of brutal shock it would take to jolt her into keen, gasping awareness of them. They frighten and excite themselves with scenarios that would make their mother cast aside her dish cloth and her laundry and come running across the beach, the street, come wading through the river to save them from drowning, strangers, drowning again.

The rotary dryer, heavy with dripping washing, shifts and grates in the breeze. Their mother is inside the caravan. They can hear her moving about, setting down lids, tapping a wooden spoon on the side of a pan. A steamy waft of boiling ham emanates from the door. Their father, of course, is not in.

'Let's show it to the holiday people first,' the eldest girl whispers, voicing the thoughts of all of them. They walk proudly and purposefully across the poorly landscaped park, past the toilet block and towards the low hedge that divides the park in two. On the far side of the hedge are the holiday people. Inside one of the large static caravans they can hear a television blaring. They knock politely, and wait.

'They can't have heard. Knock louder.'

Rap-rap-rap. It is hard to knock properly on the flimsy melamine door. They give it a couple of minutes. The telly roars and recedes like a wave on the seashore. RAP-RAP-RAP-RAP-RAP. There is a muffled boom from within and then the familiar rocking wobble of someone walking heavily along the length of a caravan. The girls step back and the door falls open towards them. A woman leans out, grasping her striped-cotton dressing gown between her flaccid breasts. Her face is deep-lined and tired and her red eyes are blinking against the brightness of the sunshine, the brightness of the white bucket that is being held out to her by one of a group of small, shabby girls.

'Yes? What is it? What d'you want?' Even as she is saying this and struggling to rise out of last night's beery fug, the woman is aware of something not quite right, something out of place and uncommon. Something dangerous. Ancient, visceral fear and an extreme physical aversion kick in with uncontrollable force from the briefest glance at the thing being held out to her, the thing that lies coiled and ready to spring.

'What the – Gerry! It's a snake! It's a bloody snake!' The woman is screaming and reaching forward, trying to grasp the handle of the door and pull it shut and at the same time desperately clutching her robe. Gerry appears behind her, filling up the doorframe, his naked torso vast and shiny with sweat. The girls don't really hear the angry words. They see the man's jowls judder and sway as the fleshy mouth chews and spits out the swear words and they watch with fascinated shock as quick ripples pass across his great gut with each furious gesture. It feels to them as though the shouting goes on for a very long time. At last, with painful finality and a last shake of his fist, the man slams the door shut and the screaming dies away. The children walk back to their own side of the hedge. They can't even look at the eel now, lying quiet and compliant in the pristine bucket thumping against their scabby knees.

* * *

The youngest girl slips into her seat next to her father and stares into her soup. He encircles her with one arm and lightly kisses the top of her head.

'Where have you been? We were worried about you.'

She shrugs. 'Nowhere.'

'Nowhere?'

'Nowhere.' Her ham and lentil soup has been sitting untouched for so long that it has separated out. Through an inch of clear salty liquid she can see an accumulation of pale chalky lentils and solid vegetable pieces in the bottom of the bowl. For some reason that she doesn't understand, she cannot bring herself to plunge her shiny spoon into the bowl and disturb the murky broth below. She leans sideways, laying her head in her father's lap, and weeps.

*   *   *

It is getting dark. They are waiting for her in the caravan. She heard the call for supper ages ago but still she can't bring herself to leave Gorilla Rock. After the thing had happened – the shout-ing thing with the holiday people – the others had got sick and tired of the eel game. They went off to the shore with some of the older children from their own side of the hedge. They left her with the bucket and the eel. Trailing the bucket back up the slope, she half-hoped the eel was a snake and would dart out and away under cover of the ferns. Except he didn't. He wasn't. He was quiet and still like a prisoner who has known for a very long time that he is going to die. When she got to it, she saw that his pool had filled up a bit but the dam was still holding out well. She looked him over one last time. He seemed less shiny now, a bit dried-out maybe. She tipped the bucket and he fell with a gentle plop into the water. It didn't take him any time at all to realise where he was. He made straight for the fist-shaped hole. And then, the shameful thing itself. Worse than the shouting holiday people. Worse, even, than being left alone in sole charge of the eel and his fate. She reached over to the opposite bank and picked up one of the discarded divining sticks: a perfect forked stick cut from a hazel tree with her father's sharpest knife. She held the smooth handles as she would if she was looking for underground water and defied the stick to pull her away from what she had to do. She had to tighten her small hands to block out the familiar gentle nodding. It felt like she was tugging herself away from the pull of a giant magnet. She got that lurching, wobbly, slippery feeling from coming too close to the source itself but she managed to wrench herself free and turned towards the eel's hidey-hole. She shoved the pointer end of the stick in hard and felt something give. She pushed it in again and again, all around the inside of the hole. Shallow water was sucking in and out of the crack and carrying out little flecks of eel skin and floating pieces of straggly gut. Throwing the stick as far away from her as she could, the little girl scrambled up the steep rock face towards the dam. She kicked it, pushed it, screamed at it with all her might until it gave with a terrifying loud rush, boulders and small stones thudding and clattering towards the oval pool below. The water raced over the sides of the pool, strewing dead moss everywhere.

She can hear them calling her again. They will be sitting down to their supper now, wondering where she is. She hopes the eel is gone; washed away forever, carried down to the sea to be nibbled into nothing by a million tiny fishes. She hopes he isn't still in the dark hole, determined to spoil their fun some other day.

Wheels

SYLVIA G PEARSON

There was little movement in the grey pall of pollution over Soweto. Pre-dawn fires had not yet been poked to life. Dogs had not begun to bark. Sipho Shabangu pulled a faded shell suit over his working clothes, zipping it all the way to hide collar and tie. His wife, Zola, handed him one trainer and continued to replace the broken lace of the other with string.

'Here is a tin of sahdines which can fit in your pocket,' she said, 'and be careful when you pass the Munyati house. I heard that Khaba did not have enough to drink in the shebeen last night, so he will be restless.'

'Good that you are telling me. The last thing we need is for that troublemahka to find out that I am wehking. I hope the strike is soon going to be over. I can't cope up with the stress of this secrecy much longer. Truly, I don't know how that Munyati and his comrades can sit around drinking while their femilies go without food.'

Sipho shot a look of concern at his four children asleep on a mattress in the corner of this one room. The oldest boy, named after him, was lying on the outer edge, one bare leg and arm exposed, the pale palm of his hand upturned and relaxed in sleep, its brown creases already testifying to chores beyond his ten years. Sipho bent down and drew the thin coverlet over his son's limbs.

'Maybe soon we can get anothah blenket. I heard that they are going cheap in that Indian shop in Eldorado.' *Tsa! – Eldorado, city of gold, eGoli – Johannesburg, golden city, and all around us here, grey, smoke-hung streets filled with grey concrete houses, asbestos in every roof, water pipes at every tenth door and electricity cut off where bills cannot be paid.*

Sipho laid the flat of his hands on his wife's hips as she stooped for stove kindling. 'See you tonight,' he said, and pulled a balaclava over his head.

There was no way he could avoid passing the Munyati house, so he jogged down the centre of the street, making use of the few tufts of grass which struggled through layers of ash and debris. His breathing rasped in the cold air. With forty minutes to spare he would take a different route the rest of the way – longer but safer. There! He was well past Khaba's house without rousing dog or owner.

He arrived at the waiting place and stood running on the spot so that the chill air would not cool his sweating skin. He could feel the damp coarseness of the wool catch on patches of jaw hair. At last the mini-bus which would take him to the railway station rattled to a halt. Sipho greeted its driver, Vuso, with enquiries about his ailing mother, his wife and children, and, finally, his own health, and climbed aboard. Vuso struggled to reply, overcome by a fresh fit of soft consumptive coughing deep in his chest.

The usual five women were the only passengers, but others could easily join the transport before they were out of Soweto's sprawling suburbs, so Sipho remained covered, his only concession – to roll up his balaclava into a cap.

'Eh-heh-heh, Sipho, how is it with the jogging these days?' cackled a woman who travelled three times a week to service luxury flats in Johannesburg.

'It is much the same, gets me from A to B and feeds the femily – and how is it with your rich bosses?'

'Ach, truly they ah ovahfed! They talk about us Africans, but have you seen some of thoz beeg white Jewish meddems? They have bellies like bean begs and breasts like train bumpahs. And when they get in the gahden chair I wait for the creck, heh-heh-heh! Their necks ah so heavy with gold chains, and their rings – have you seen them? Diamonds like bicycle lamps, I'm telling you. Can you believe it – all that money and being so sad that the skin of their faces is pulled down to lie in folds around their necks. They look like turtles with a bad smell undah their noses – and no eggs to lay!'

Sipho had heard it all before, variations on a theme which produced endless mirth among the passengers. He settled, safe in the knowledge that they were sympathisers whose men, like him, had defied Cosatu Union strike rules.

There were two things he must do today. He must ask his boss at the Office Stationery factory for a rise in pay. In his lunch break he must go to the nearby shopping mall and bargain with the Craft Shop madam over those wire model bicycles he supplied to her. Strange what some Whites would buy, bits of wire, off-cuts from binder machines, twisted into shape. Since Mandela's release, Black Consciousness had ballooned and there was an increasing demand for artefacts from Soweto. Sipho was not the only one who made these, but his were the best, fashioned from *new* wire. Others used spokes from wheels of wrecked cycles, while some were bad and bold enough to remove their material from perfectly sound ones parked outside shops or houses. Sipho's models were eight inches long and four and a half high. The wheels moved, the handlebars were sturdy, with brakes and a place for a water bottle. He had even made tiny props so that they could be stood up – perfect miniatures of the real thing in Soweto's big Bicycle Shop.

He had just put the finishing touches to the last two dozen, filing down rough edges, squinting along their lengths for telltale signs of a buckled wheel, and even brightening the frames with steel wool and paraffin-dipped rags till they shone like newly minted coins. Now each one was wrapped in newspaper and tightly packed in a Nestlé's condensed milk carton stowed behind the stove at home. There they would remain until the strike was over and he could take them to Johannesburg. Whites, who bought them for display on shelves in their homes, paid eleven rands 75 cents, while he received three rands 95 – a large difference which he hoped to shrink by at least another rand or two when he saw the madam today.

Once aboard the train, Sipho leaned against his corner window seat and relaxed into the rocking rhythm. In half an hour he would see the first outlines of Johannesburg's tall buildings as the sun started to bleed into the sky. He thought about his boss, Johan Pretorius, and how he would approach him. He must remember to be polite but firm, not dog-like as some of his fellow workers were, shuffling, staring at their feet, twisting hands behind backs. Johan Pretorius was a fair man since long before the freeing of Mandela, not foul-mouthed and physical like some Whites. *Kaffir* was a term which never spilled from his lips. And he used their *real* names, their African ones. But he had a difficult face to read, for he seldom smiled and moreover his features were lost in a huge beard bushing over jaw and neck, and crawling out of sight inside his shirt.

At the railway station Sipho fought his way through the crowds spewing from every door of the train, and slipped into a toilet booth. He peeled off his shell suit, rolled it into a tight wad and used it to flick the dust of Soweto from his shoes before tucking it under his arm.

Inside the factory, halfway through the morning, the tea-break bell screamed in his ear, its echo bouncing along the lines of many unmanned machines. Sipho laid the tin of sardines and a penknife on his bench. He was hungry after a cold breakfast of bread dipped in some gravy saved from last night's meal. His head felt light, as though it would sail off his shoulders if he shook it. The food would make him feel better, and after a mug of sweet tea in the canteen he would take his place in the queue to see his boss, secure in the knowledge that he was well up on his morning's quota.

He was about to pierce the sardine tin when he saw Johan Pretorius striding across the factory floor towards him. As usual, the White man's lips were a grim line, just discernible in the face of hair. Sipho's heart swerved. His boss so seldom approached any of the machine operators. What had he done wrong? He could not think of anything. Had someone leaked it to his boss that he was going to ask for a rise? And was Johan Pretorius angry – with enough worries on his plate? Sipho folded his knife and pocketed it with the tin. A sour taste filled his mouth as his boss's huge hairy hand came down on his shoulder.

'A word with you Shabangu, in my office – right now!' Sipho followed Johan Pretorius, stomach knotted and gurgling with emptiness. He pressed a fist into his belly. There was a tray on his boss's red leather-covered desk, with a tall copper jug, two cups and saucers, a bowl of coloured sugar and a plate of biscuits. He watched with big eyes as his boss poured steaming black coffee from the pot and slid a cup towards him.

'Sit down, Shabangu, sit down.'

Sipho sipped carefully, afraid to make his African noises. The White man leaned back in his high chair, lifted a Zebra-striped box and drew with finger and thumb from its sheath of black tissue a wire bicycle model measuring eight by four and a half inches.

'You make these, Shabangu? And sell them to the Craft Shop in the mall? For 3 rands 95?'

Sipho nodded, could not find his voice. Had his foreman misinformed him that it was okay to use the wire off-cuts, that no one would object? Sipho forgot his hunger, feeding all his energy into anxiety. How had Johan Pretorius come by one of his bicycles, and what were all those questions about?

As though reading his thoughts, the bearded man's face split in a broad smile, two gold-capped incisors flashing. 'She's a friend of mine – your Craft Shop madam – asked me what's 'appened to you, it's two months since your last consignment. We got talking. I was telling her about your loyalty to me during this *blerry* strike – loyalty in the face of some nawsty retaliation if you found out – I'm right on this, Shabangu, *ja*?'

Sipho nodded.

'I got thinking about all this work you putting into bits of wire from the scrap heap – and for only three ninety five a time, hey? And you not much richer at the end of the day, hey?'

Sipho, encouraged by his boss's friendly tone said, 'No, boss, you ah right. My wife, she jokes with me that with *all* my bicycles I do not get very fah, heh-heh.'

'Exactly, Shabangu. *Exactly.*'

Sipho watched the big man lean towards him, hands making twin bridges on the desktop.

'You a smart man, Shabangu. The popularity of those models from Soweto is on the increase and you saw your chance, and even improved on them. Now the demand is greater than the supply. It's a lesson to me. We business people need to ah . . . diversify.' He narrowed his eyes. 'And that's where you come in,

Shabangu. Let's test the market as of next week, put you and your wheels on the road, so to speak.' He gave a short explosive laugh at his own joke and Sipho responded with a grin. 'What do you say to a place of your own – over there in the machine shop? We can clear out the unused equipment that's just lying around gathering dust – and you can have as much wire as you want. Do some drawings for me, Shabangu, and who knows what we'll come up with? Use your initiative. Expand your repertoire with novel ideas. Be inventive, adventurous.' Sipho waited while the White man took a mouthful of coffee and wiped his upper lip with a blue handkerchief, but he did not know what to say. He did not understand all of those big words, was mystified by Johan Pretorius's enthusiasm. His boss pushed the plate of biscuits towards him.

''Elp yourself, Sipho.' *Sipho*!

He reached out and took three shiny wrapped rectangles, red, silver, gold, immediately feeling ashamed of doubting such a generous man. As he bit into the layers of chocolate and caramel, aware that his saliva could betray him, Johan continued with his spiel, but in such a quiet voice that Sipho had to stop crunching in case he missed something.

'Try a saxophone, Sipho. I saw a *lekker*[1] specimen at a roadside craft stall – five feet tall. And a *klein*[2] bi-plane made from flattened Schweppes cans. You could do it. You've got the eye. Once we see how your prototypes are received by the retail trade we can talk about a cut for you . . .' He paused, searching Sipho's face with blazing eyes. 'A percentage on the wholesale price,' he added, the tip of his tongue circling his lips.

[1] nice (Afrikaans)
[2] little (Africaans)

Sipho hardly dared believe what he was hearing, nodding so hard that his head would surely fall off. Johan Pretorius was reaching across for his hand. He felt the hard squeeze of the paw – an *African* hand-shake – and was charged with enough energy to speak.

'Thenk you boss, thenk you verry, verry much – heh-heh, looks like my bicycles are going to get me somewheah aftah all, neh?'

'*Ja*, Shabangu, you said it. Wheels, man!' Once again Shabangu saw a glint of gold in the White man's smile. 'Wheels within wheels, Shabangu, and who knows where they will take us, hey?'

A Softer Devil

DEREK ROBERTSON

Toby Greer shot the dog that always barked at him when he came home from school. He used his grandfather's rifle, taking aim from his upper bedroom window. It was a warm sunny afternoon, everything bright and clear, and he didn't try and hide anything. When the patrol car rolled up it didn't take a genius to work out where the fatal shot came from; Toby watched as the two cops stood on the opposite lawn, the dog lying dead at their feet, as both of them shielded their eyes against the sun and looked up towards his room. He felt like giving them a little wave but thought better of it. He wasn't that crazy. They took him down to the station, and after some court business, put him on the juvenile offenders' programme.

The one question everyone kept asking was, Why? Why did you do it, Toby? This was asked so many times, and in so many different ways, that Toby started to categorise each particular question according to his own classification system. It all started in the cruiser taking him to the station: 'Why did you do it, fuck-face? What did that poor animal ever do to you, you sick little bastard?' Toby later wrote this up in a little ragged note-book as:

> *Thursday July 14th fat cop in police car*
> *aggressive/impotent/phony*

Toby set this notebook on fire when the court-appointed psychiatrist started to sniff around and afterwards he kept all of this stuff in his head. Toby hadn't been in trouble before, so although his misdemeanour involved use of a deadly firearm, he was put on the State's first offender programme. So, all right, he wasn't going to get the lethal jab up in Bartlett, or have his cute little orange-suited butt on parade in detention, but to a withdrawn, awkward fifteen-year-old, some things can seem just as bad. Like having to make that phone call to his mother.

'Ma, I'm in trouble with the cops, they're asking me who'll be my guardian . . .'

'Fuck, Toby, just tell me what you've done.'

'I shot a dog.'

'A dog. You killed a dog? What kinda dog? Fuckin' Jesus. What's wrong with you, Toby?'

'They're asking who'll come and sit with me; to make sure I understand everything and so nobody takes advantage.'

There was silence from the other end of the line.

'Mother?'

'I can't do this Toby. I've got my own problems with Jack and I'm not travelling all that way just to hold your hand. It's impossible. You know how it is, Toby, you damned well know how it is.'

Two years before Toby's mother had high-tailed it off to Sacramento with Jack. She'd known Jack for exactly eight days prior to their departure. Sure, crazy love can make people do some foolish things, but there's a difference between being a fool and being a shit. Being a shit means leaving your son standing by the sidewalk as you leave with a stranger in a beat-up station wagon, and you don't turn around, and you don't say where you're going or when, or if you'll ever call.

Toby hated putting his grandmother and grandfather through all this rehab-parole stuff. They were so old and frail and until this their lives had been quiet and decent. Toby would watch them as they listened to all of the official stuff, the legal jargon and head-babble, like Oprah, only times a thousand. They always looked ready for crying, their bewildered eyes liquid with restrained tears; their old liver-spotted hands white with tension. Jesus, he was a total asshole.

And all of this was just the start, the whole set-up seemed to have been thought up by a sadist, some guy who'd spent years studying adolescents, boys just like Toby Greer, discovering their weak points, their secret terrors, all those dark things that lie hidden, buried for very good reasons. We're here to discover why you're so angry, Toby. At that moment, can you tell us what you were feeling? Do you feel any resentment towards your mother? Do you find it hard to love people, Toby, is that a real problem for you? And of course, why did you do it, Toby?

October 22nd counsellor with fake hair friendly/sneaky/routine

Toby hated the talk, all those words, the search for explanations, for reasons. He remembered the time when his mother would ask him things: why don't you like carrots, Toby, everyone likes carrots, why don't you? So, maybe mothers were allowed to ask questions. But these guys; with their tape recorders and note-books, writing everything down, looking up if he said something stupid. Just because, Toby wanted to say, just because.

The very worst moment was when they made him meet the people who owned the dog. This was so Toby would under-stand the seriousness of his crime, give him a chance to apologise, and help everyone with closure – it was the counsel-lor's word – on this whole sorry business. It didn't seem like a good idea to Toby.

They were neighbours who lived directly across the street from Toby's grandparents' house. But Toby had never spoken to them before, nor had he ever really noticed them either. It was always just that noisy howling dog, tied up to a kennel post in the garden, pacing up and down, all day and every day, always straining to get over that fence to bite your ass off.

So Toby was surprised when he was led into the room to see how young they were, not any more than twenty-five. They were sitting on two of the four chairs placed in the centre of the room in a rectangle of two-by-two intimacy. The couple were dressed in casual weekend clothes, checked shirt and chinos for him, white blouse and jeans for her. And Toby immediately recognised her as a babe, one of those bright, clean women that all the guys in Toby's class used to dream about, the ones with the heart-tugging smiles and blow-job lips. Toby Greer was a total shit, no mistake now. Guided by the counsellor Toby was directed into one of the chairs opposite the young couple. Each pair faced the other directly, so close that they could, if they wanted to, stretch out a foot and touch the person opposite. Or maybe kick the person in the mouth and break their jaw and stamp on their dog-killing face.

'Mr and Mrs Henshaw, this is Toby Greer, the boy who killed your dog. Would either of you like to say anything to Toby about how you feel or what this has all meant to you?'

Toby would have preferred to look away but that would have been too disrespectful, so he sat upright in his chair looking directly at them, ready for whatever they had to throw at him. And they had the right. But before a word was spoken Mrs Henshaw began to cry; slow, silent tears ran down that beautiful face and Toby nearly couldn't take it. Right now, Toby needed her husband to get up and kill him, to make him feel pain, to make him bleed. But all Mr Henshaw did was put his arm around his wife and pull her close.

'I'm sorry, I didn't mean to cause you any trouble; I just fucked up.'

The counsellor gave Toby a sign that he should leave now and he started to get up. As Toby was leaving Mr Henshaw turned away from his wife's bowed head and said, 'You've the devil in you son, and that's only ever going to lead one way.'

Toby didn't believe that Cain and Abel shit, although half of Texas did, and maybe even Mr Henshaw did. But it played on his mind, stuck there like a bad-conscious itch. After all the talk and analysis the world seemed happy with the conclusion that Toby Greer was just plain bad, and somewhere, sometime along the line he would get what he deserved. And you saw it in the way people looked at him, even his grandparents, looks that said you're already a hopeless case, beyond our or anyone's help, a true failure and a total fuck-up.

Near the end of his rehab they threw Toby in among the other lost boys. It was just like the remedial class in school, a garbage dump for the halt and lame. Each Wednesday and Friday they would meet down at the juvenile probation office. There would be eight to ten boys and a single, pissed-off probation officer. This was the twilight detail and you could just see how pleased the guy was, having to baby-sit ten worthless pieces of adolescent shit. They would all sit in a big circle of chairs and there seemed to be some kind of competition going on as to who could slouch the most and who could send off the strongest fuck-you vibe. Toby would always sit beside a Mexican who wore a white vest showing off his body-builder arms and gang-tattoos and who never spoke during the entire time they were in there. He looked plenty though, and Toby thought those looks were the most eloquent, expressive things he ever heard or saw in that place.

'He was messing with my girl, man, you know what I'm saying.'

'There's been drugs in my house since I was five years old; what do you mean I should stay away from that kinda stuff?'

'You shot a dog? Are you fuckin' crazy?'

But everyone knew that this room was the end. That it was a staging post on the way to more crime and more prison, and for lives that were going nowhere. Toby would look around the room and he would try and figure which of them would be dead before they were thirty. They weren't going to be having any class reunion, that's for sure.

For the last week of the probation programme the juvenile offenders were sent off to the local churches to do some low-skilled maintenance work. The hope was that some priest or pastor could say something to them that might turn them around. It was like saying we've done as much as we can for you boys, but here's some last minute advice from God before we send you out into the world again. Toby was down for some painting work at the Pentecostal Church on Fulton Street. There were three other boys and they were to be supervised by a weedy little guy named Herbert Johnson who they soon agreed to call 'The Invisible Man'. Toby would always remember his grandparents on that first church morning. It was like they were sending their son to his first day at school, both of them full of hope and expectation, thinking that this was the start of something good. Jesus, it tore him up. Five days with a paintbrush in his hand wasn't going to change a thing, it just doesn't work like that.

The church was an old clapboard building which had been put up during the 1930s. It didn't look in need of any painting whatsoever, and Toby thought that it must be one of the best maintained churches in the world, there being lots of JOs available for the work. The boys fooled around as they waited for the man who was going to help them put up the scaffolding platform. Weedy Herbert Johnson wasn't enough of an expert on this and they had to wait for the specialist.

'And listen, when that Pastor puts his hand on your knee, you better scream that you love the Lord or else your sweet ass will be in danger, mortal danger.'

'My brother tells me that they'll be rolling around on the floor come Sunday speaking in tongues and kissing rattlesnakes. Have you ever kissed a snake, Greer, or are you an out and out dog guy?'

A big flat-bed truck brought in the scaffolding and two guys got out; they were dressed like rodeo riders and both wore white Stetsons. They shook hands with Herbert Johnson and the three of them stood to have a smoke. When they finished their smokes Herbert Johnson just walked off without a backward glance, and the boys wouldn't see him for another two days. One of the pair got some things out of the truck and the two men started to walk towards the boys who were acting cool by lounging on the front lawn of the church. 'Here comes the cavalry,' said Ramirez, giving the others a big grin and showing off his gold fillings.

The two cowboys stood over the boys and gave them the stare.

'This is Tony, and I'm Pete. We're here to teach you how to build scaffold. Just two things you need to know: one, him and me is the boss; two, you four are the grunts. Got that?' Tony then fired a pair of heavy canvas gloves at each of the boys and everyone knew the kidding was done. For the whole of that morning they took the poles and boards off the flat-bed and walked them into the church. It was hard in the heat and no one said they could take a break till it was all done. Toby's t-shirt was soaked in sweat and his arms were aching as he collapsed into the pews of the church when the lifting was finished.

'Girls, that's what they are, Tony, lovely delicate girls.' Even Ramirez was too tired for a wisecrack. 'We're now going to take those poles and boards and make us a scaffold. We're going to go way up there,' if the boys had had the strength to look they would have seen him pointing to the cornice of the church ceiling, 'eighteen feet if I'm not mistaken.'

'Now you four have probably never made a decent job of anything in your whole miserable lives, huh? This is where you start. My ass, and my friend Pete's ass, and your pretty little worthless asses are all on the line up there and we can't be having any trashy workmanship here. I'll be checking every cleat and clamp as we go and if I find any one of you is messing up then you're gone; back on parole, week one, listening to all those suits badmouthing you again. Comprende?'

Toby thought they sounded like something out of one of those Vietnam war films; the tough sergeant speaking to the raw, callow recruits, the boys who would soon be men. Or dead.

But they soon got the rhythm of the task, they began to grasp the logic of the structure, how it was fitting together, how it grew tall, how the poles were joined and the boards laid firm. They were learning to test the clamps with the pull of a gloved hand and to stamp their feet to sound out the solidity of the boards. They became experts in throwing clamps from one level to the next and they sensed the waiting shame for any fool who ever dropped one. By the end of that first day they had a pretty good start to a proper scaffold. Toby left the church exhausted but he knew there was still work to be done tomorrow and he was glad of that, although he didn't let on to any of the others.

The next day they all fell in quickly with the work. The Invisible Man was due to arrive with the paint after lunch and there was no time to waste. Toby found himself working with Pete laying down the top-level duckboards. The others were down below making sure the access ladders were secure.

Pete just said it out of nowhere, 'Do you believe in the church, Toby?'

Toby thought Pete was setting up some sort of joke and he gave him the Ramirez line, 'We're all waiting for the preacher to show up to send us straight to Hell.' Pete paused before saying, 'The pastor's a good man; he might put you straight on some things.' Oh Jesus, thought Toby, not this, not the born-again shit, don't give me that. Pete lifted up one end of the last plank and nodded to Toby to take up the other end. They held it over the last vacant space and then dropped it into place. Pete gave it the ritual stomp his end and then nodded to Toby, a big smile breaking over his face. Toby couldn't help but smile back and stomped his own foot down on the board; he stomped it hard.

'And I will give unto every one of you according to your works,' Pete said. Toby gripped the guardrail with his gloved hand and pushed and pulled with all his strength. Nothing moved; the structure was sound.

I know something you don't know

ALI SMITH

The boy had come home from school one lunchtime in May and gone to his bed. He'd been every day in his bed now for nearly four months, all the bad summer. In those early weeks he had still made the effort to sit up in the morning when she went in to open the curtains. For the past couple of weeks all he'd done was open his eyes, not even moving his head on the pillow.

It was a condition which didn't show up on tests. It was most likely a post-viral condition. Three different doctors had seen him: the GP, a consultant paediatrician at the hospital and, last month, a different, private, top consultant paediatrician who held clinics in one of the big houses in the rich part of the city, did all the same tests on the boy's feet and hands, looked into his eyes and ears, took blood. The results had been inconclusive and had cost £800. Now it was August. When she had gone into his room to open the curtains this morning he'd kept his eyes shut and in a small voice from the bed had said: please don't.

The boy's mother went into the kitchen and got out the Yellow Pages.

Under Healers it said See Complementary Therapies.

Complementary Therapies was between Compensation Claims and Composts, Peats and Mulches. Only two of the therapists listed were local. One was called Heavenly Health Analysis Ltd. Complimentary health care treatment, holistic health screening. Inner journey Indian head massage. Stress, worries.

Hopi candle ear wax removal. Herbal advice line, health problems etc. Outstanding accurate understanding from qualified registered therapist Karen Pretty.

The other advertising box had only three words in it and a number.

Nicole. Trust Me. 260223.

The boy's mother dialled the first number. It was a machine. There was music. A calm singsong voice over the top of the music said Hello caller. You are welcome. Be sure to leave your details, including the important information of how you found this contact number for Heavenly Health Analysis Ltd, after the tone.

Hello, she said. I found your details in the Yellow Pages. I would be very much obliged if you could call me back regarding a serious health matter.

She dialled the second number. She let the phone ring in case an answerphone had to be activated. It rang thirty times. When she took it away from her ear and held it up in front of her to press the end of calls button, a tiny distant word shot out of the plastic in her hand.

What?

Eh, hello? the boy's mother said.

Yes, what? the voice said in her ear.

I'm trying to get in touch with a person called Nicole, the boy's mother said. I was looking –

Come on, for Christ's sake, what? the voice said.

It's my son, she said.

I charge fifty pounds a visit, the voice said.

Yes, the boy's mother said.

Where do you live? the voice said. Hurry up. I really need to go to the toilet.

The boy's mother told the voice the address and where to turn right at the roundabout if coming by car but the voice had hung up, she couldn't tell when, somewhere in the list of directions, and she was left saying hello? into the phone, to nobody.

Before she'd had to stay at home all day because of the boy, she had been an assistant clerk in the office of a company which made a lot of money installing digital phone networks all over the third world. The third world was still open territory for phones. The company also set up cheap mobile deals with Eastern European countries using second-hand mobiles people traded in for updated phones here in the West. Voices all over Eastern Europe were talking on old UK phones; this was something she'd liked to think about, before. It was a funny and interesting thought that someone with a different life and a totally incomprehensible language (to her) might be talking to someone, arguing with someone, whispering secrets or sorting everyday things about shopping or family down what might be her old phone.

But it wasn't amusing to think anymore, not in the same way, now that what she talked about down her own phone to her mother or to the people from work, were things she didn't really want to hear come out of her mouth, about what the boy wasn't doing, like eating much today. Or wanting to watch TV, even the cartoons. Or letting himself be got up without a fuss so he could go through to the bathroom. Or even responding at all anymore when she sat on his bed and asked him questions: do you want to watch the cartoons? Will I put the football video in? Is it sore in your arms? Is it sore in your eyes? Is it sore in your head? Where in your head? Too bright? Too dark? Do you want the light on? Off?

The phone in her hand rang. Caller unknown. She watched it ring.

She let it click into answerphone then waited for it to tell her that it had received a new message. She played the message back. It was the voice of Karen Pretty from Heavenly; it offered three initial consultation times.

The boy's mother phoned back and left her choice on the Heavenly answerphone.

The doorbell rang. It was after lunch, after the boy had shrunk back into the sheets away from the plate saying he was too cold, and after she'd sat at the dining room table downstairs and eaten, herself, the two fish fingers and the microwave chips she'd put on the plate for him.

There was a rough-looking woman at the door. She was middle-aged and sloppily dressed in a stained long t-shirt and black leggings.

Fifty up front, cash, the woman said. Where's the, what's it again, a boy? Is he in his bed?

She had her foot in the door. The boy's mother explained, holding the door, that she'd engaged someone else.

Yeah, right, the woman said. Karen Pretty, ear wax queen, is it? Can't even spell complementary medicine right and you're letting her near something you love. I wouldn't. Each to their own. Just remember if she comes. Karen Pretty. KP Nuts is what I call her.

The woman had got into the house. She was standing in the hall now, looking past the boy's mother up the stairs.

I'll take a cheque if it's made out to cash, she said on her way up. Her bulk made the stairwell look small. She held her hand out to keep the boy's mother at the foot of the stairs. She breathed like a heavy smoker; her breath was audible over the traffic noise through the open door.

Be down in a minute, she said. Hurry with that cheque, will you?

It was true; it was only about a minute, maybe even less, before she was wheezing down again and standing in the doorway of the sitting room.

I've no idea what's wrong with him, she said. He'll probably be okay. By the way, can I get a glass of water?

The boy's mother went to the kitchen and filled a beer glass with tap water. When she came back the front door was shut, the cheque had gone from the arm of the armchair with the chequebook and the bankcard, there was no sign of the woman anywhere up or down the street outside the house and it wasn't till half an hour later when she looked for her handbag that she realised it was gone as well and so were the two Capo Di Monte figurines, gone from the windowsill.

Seated Lady and Child. Clown Balancing a Ball.

Karen Pretty from Heavenly Health Analysis Ltd came at the appointed time two days later even though the boy's mother had cancelled her by answerphone. She was on crutches. She stood precariously on the rug in the middle of the sitting room.

Do you have a hard upright chair? she said. Like a dining room chair? Thank you very much. I'd just like to make it clear to you that I don't intend to charge for this visit because it is an initial consultation visit. Can you put it exactly here?

She drew a line on the floor with the end of a crutch.

Bless you, she said.

She was too young to say bless you. She looked about twenty-five. She had long brown hair held back with a clasp at the nape of her neck. She looked familiar to the boy's mother.

Do you not work at the Abbey National? she asked the girl.

Karen Pretty put her crutches neatly together, held them in the one hand and sat down in the middle of the room.

You probably know by now that Nicole Campbell of Trust Me is in the process of being prosecuted by the CPS for fraud, she said. I feel for you, Mrs Haig, what's your first name please?

Harriet, the boy's mother said.

I can feel you are carrying pain, Harriet, Karen Pretty said. I feel that someone full of sadness lives in this house.

Karen Pretty, eyes closed, smiled and nodded.

White, she said or maybe, Quite.

Are you going to be able to get upstairs? the boy's mother said. Only, that's where he is.

Where who is? Karen Pretty said still with her eyes shut.

My son. Anthony. He's the one who's ill, the boy's mother said.

Yes. Somehow I sensed, Karen Pretty said, that I would be doing a tarot reading for a boy who couldn't get down some stairs today.

She opened her eyes, looked into her shoulder bag, took something out and held it up.

I could carry him down, the boy's mother said.

Oh no, we don't actually need him actually bodily in the room with us, Karen Pretty said.

She unwrapped a little wooden box from inside a swathe of red silk.

I charge thirty pounds per reading, she said. But I intend not to charge you, Harriet, for today's session. The guides have asked me not to.

The Girl Guides? the boy's mother thought. She imagined them all in the uniforms of her own childhood, shaking their heads at her.

They say you will remember this kindness, and repay my kindness amply in the future with your own kindness, Karen Pretty said.

No, I'd much prefer to – the boy's mother said.

He is carrying pain, Karen Pretty suddenly said. His spirit is very strong. Is he a headstrong kind of a boy?

Well, no, the boy's mother said, not really.

Yes, that's right, Karen Pretty said.

Karen Pretty and the boy's mother sat in silence for half a minute or so. It felt like a very long time. It was long enough to feel embarrassing. Then Karen Pretty put her hand out and presented a worn pack of cards to the boy's mother.

Your mother is going to shuffle them for you, Anthony, she said to the fireplace.

The boy's mother blushed. She shuffled the cards and handed them back to Karen Pretty who turned one up, then the next, then the next and laid them out beside each other on her knees.

A struggle for position will end in improvement, she said pointing at the boy on top of a hill with a stick, fighting off a lot of people below him with sticks. A difficult journey to a calmer place, she said pointing at the boat full of swords in the water. A reawakening, she said pointing to the family climbing out of a grave beneath a giant set of wings. I am not going to charge you the usual thirty pounds for this reading, she said gathering the cards and putting the pack together again. The boy's mother insisted. She gave Karen Pretty two folded twenties. Karen Pretty took the money and put it down on the carpet by the chair leg. She called a taxi firm on her mobile. The two women sat in silence while they waited. Karen Pretty smiled a sweet smile at the boy's mother and shrugged her eyebrows high into her forehead. She sighed. She hummed a tune. She was patient as if patience was a part of her remit.

Peace to you, Harriet, she said when the taxi drew up outside the house.

She leaned on her crutches to get herself to her feet. The boy's mother watched her back herself onto the seat of the taxi and watched the taxi drive away. She looked round the room, in which there was more than a trace of Karen Pretty's perfume. She opened the window to get rid of it.

She put the dining room chair back in the dining room. She kicked the folded money across the carpet till it disappeared under the sofa.

She went upstairs to check. He was asleep. His short out-breaths made her own breathing hurt.

That night, though she'd undressed herself and got into bed, she made herself get up again and come downstairs. In the kitchen, over the sink, she struck a safety match and set the two twenty-pound notes alight together and held them so they burned all the way to the tips of her fingers, flushed the black stuff they left down the sink then wiped the sink clean and dry with the tea-towel. She went back to bed. She realised she had forgotten to check on him like she always did at the top of the stairs. She got up. She stood at the crack in the door and saw his head on the pillow in the dark.

She lay in bed with the light off and her eyes wide open because this time, she knew, she'd really been robbed of something. But this time she couldn't be totally sure what it was.

The boy was in bed. It had been days and days. It was September. His mother had come in to do the curtains for the morning again and he had let her.

He could see from here a whiteness which was really the side of one of the houses opposite. But it looked like snow. It was snow. It was a wide square of snow, the size of a house, snow even though it was summer.

He watched to see if it would melt, because the morning sun was sending a squinted rectangle of yellow through the gaps in the houses on his own side of the street on to the white. But the snow was super-snow, mega-strength multi-snow. No sun could melt it. If you picked it up to mould it into a snowball would it be cold on your hands or warm? A warm snowball. It would be impossible.

The boy was tired. All this thinking of snow was making him tired.

But now he was thinking of how you would make a snow-ball out of warm snow and your bare hands would stay their usual colour and not get cold or red in the process.

The bear was at the bottom of the bed. It was the big bear, the one his father had brought back years ago, when he'd flown back from work. The bear had come from an airport. It was huge. It was Ukrainian. It was nearly the same size as the boy.

He reached out in front of him until it was like his hand was touching the white square he could see through the window. It was snow. He took some of the snow in his hand. Because it was warmed snow it didn't feel unpleasant to touch. He took his other hand out from under the covers and used both hands to mould the snowball. Then he aimed it at the bear at the bottom of the bed and threw it.

The boy's arm hurt a little from the throw.

He put it back in under the covers.

Next thing he'd do was: he would shift out of the bed when the bear least expected it and sneak up without it noticing and punch the bear right in the mouth. Then he would wrestle it. Though it would fight back hard, he'd beat it. He'd kick it. He'd bite it in the ear. He'd eat the bear.

He'd totally beat it completely till it roared that it gave in.

Yesterday if he'd thought he'd wrestle a bear or make a snowball or something like that it would have made his head go the sore empty way, not like snow was a white place on an opposite wall, or summer snow, but like there was only snow, nothing else, no bed, no room, no bear, no curtains, no nothing, nothing but being in it, everything sort of snow.

But today he shifted a little out of the covers, quietly so the bear wouldn't suspect anything.

He began to feel a bit hungry.

He slid a little further out, then a little, careful, more.

Over the Counter

FRANCES WATT

Not long after nine Billy B drifts in like thin sleet on a north wind, and leaves the shop door ajar behind him. The draught dislodges tinsel in the window display, ruffles the pharmacy queue already roosting in corners between the gondolas.

Everyone knows it's Billy, from his first glottal sniff and swallow in the doorway – even Mr Em, stooped over the dispensary bench with his back to the hatch, knows Billy's arrived long before he's reached the counter. Rose starts talking at him before she looks up from the till. *Four o'clock's the time, as you well know, Billy. Mr Em's busy just now.* She enunciates this as though for a customer deaf, incapable or foreign, though Billy's none of these. Mr Em notices the angle of his own back, straightens, tries to stretch away the tension. He puts a hand up to the nape of his neck and locates the root of his headache. Yes . . . ah . . . there.

This morning, Billy's not giving up easily. A more emphatic sniff and swallow, like some throaty verbal tic, precedes a burst of eloquence. *Naw, but I'm desperate ken. I keep telling ye, I'm runnin behind – I drapped the bottle but they'll no believe me . . .* Without looking round, Mr Em knows the shrug that accompanies this; more squirm than shrug, bony shoulders lifting inside the dun-coloured parka. Billy B's been on supervision with them all week, almost family now. Steel in Rose's voice. *We can't have other customers inconvenienced by you comin in here whenever you feel like it. Billy. Four o'clock.* By the retreating phlegmy sniff and swallow Mr Em charts Billy's departure.

The queue shuffles its feathers in the wind and settles again as the door closes. *The state o that* says a voice, Mrs Dalry's. *'S a disgrace, thae junkies.* Screened from view, Mr Em looks down at the prescription in his hand. Paracetamol and laxative, bullied out of Dr Armstrong, on repeat prescription for months now. Price retail, £2.70. Prescription administration, somewhere well north of £30. He moves Mrs Dalry to the bottom of the pile. Beyond the hatch Rose interrogates the shop at large. *Next – or are you all just waiting?* Rose doesn't like anyone else criticising Billy.

Mr Em holds the next script in one hand, steadying his wrist with the other until the print clumps together into something legible and multi-syllabled. Joy J. The morphine dosage has doubled in barely two weeks. *Arsehole* he murmurs. Through the hatch he looks for Joy's dad and finds him standing in the corner staring at corn plasters and insoles; hardly more than a grey-faced boy himself and yet somehow with a dying daughter. *Bastard arsehole.*

Rose appears at his elbow like a peroxide-blonde robin, looking sideways.

Who you swearin at?

No-one.

Oh, that'll help, says Rose. *You get your cuppie now an I'll type labels. We've wee Laura today and Maggie'll be back from the surgeries in a minute.*

Wee Laura, recalled from avoiding customers at the perfume shelves, brings the reek of Poison down to the till with her. *Can I help?* she whispers, gleaming, terrified. Three voices answer.

Packet o Alka Seltzer, pal.

I think you'll find there's a queue . . .

Excuse me!

The staffroom door slices the voices off. Mr Em, careful in these things as in most others, shuts the gents' toilet door for a re-examination of his professional ethics. *The therapeutic management of dependency – long-term interventions and counter-indicators.* He puts up no argument on counter-indicators this morning.

Then tea. Mr Em appreciates what sweet tea, drunk too fast and too hot, does to the soft tissue of gullet and oesophagus and why his ulcer, self-diagnosed, complains most mid-morning. He has also a practical understanding of the effect of topical warmth on blood absorption rates.

At last, at last, the glow kicks in. Warmth to the finger-tips, an explosion of possibilities and dimensions. Mr Em stands upright at the counter where kettle, teabag box and digestive biscuit tin occupy the equidistant places Rose had allotted them. With the sharp focus that comes when his headaches lift he looks down at his own hands. One is cupped around the other, holding his mug steady in what suddenly looks like a parody of prayer, and he sees them in the way he sometimes sees the hands of customers at the counter. Billy B's hands for example – square, bony, raw-knuckled – less pale, would be a farmer's hands. And he's watched, vaguely uneasy, as the vast Mrs Dalry curls plump courtesan's fingers over change in his palm. His own hands, he judges, are now in structure finer than sits well with the rest of his person. Only the skin texture matches the self he is resigned to; liver-spotted and fine-hatched, a loop on each wrist where the cuffs of plastic gloves make indents that scarcely disappear overnight. Mr Em loosens his grip a little, and drinks deeply.

Will you take early denner today? Rose flicks at the kettle, stoops to the fridge, opens the biscuits. The high heels bring her to his shoulder. *I've chipolatas to collect. It'll let you build up an appetite for wir tea out.* Mr Em nods. Another Saturday settles into routine.

At 1.45, Billy B is back and no Rose to deflect him. Mr Em, sorting scripts, cataloguing the living and some dyings, this time does not register his arrival. Wee Laura, well coached, is dismissive. *I'm sorry, you'll have to come back later . . .*

Then Billy's voice, loud. *It's later already. It's nearly fuckin tea time. I cannae come ony later than this, it's fuckin Christmas Eve!*

Mr Em is surprised at his own speed. *Mr Em?* says Laura, voice wobbling, at the dispensary door but he's already looking round her. What is it that's out of the ordinary? Not the *fuckin's* surely? Billy is holding something in one hand inside his parka, the other lies curled too casually on the plastic counter top. Sweat on Billy's face matched by clamminess in the palm of his own hands. *You look out the afternoon deliveries, Laura* he instructs calmly.

I cannae wait till later, Billy says more quietly. *I cannae. I'm aff ma heid. Look at me.* Mr Em looks. A yellow stain down the zip edge of the parka. And Billy has stopped squirming. Mr Em notices for the first time a spatter of freckles against his ash-white cheeks. He sighs. *Come through. Come through the back.*

One sprout has a neat crystallised heart of ice inside its overlapping green scales and Rose negotiates £10 off the bill. Mr Em hands it over to Maggie and Wee Laura, for The Clubbin. On the pavement outside the two young ones ease backwards, bashful and pink-cheeked. Not for his benefit the tattoos displayed tonight above the exposed rims of their underwear. Only Rose rises off her stilletos to meet his stoop. Youth Dew engulfs him. *Thanks for the present, Mr Em. Yes – thanks, Mr Em. Merry Christmas! Merry Christmas! Chee'o, Chee'o,* And Rose, looking back from the corner. *You will get a taxi?*

Yes Rose, he says, sober as Saturday morning on a bottle of Merlot and two brandies. Mist sits above the eaves of the Town House, pats magic from the Christmas lights. He reaches for his hip-flask.

Mr Chemist Mannie! Billy B's voice. *You look different wi no white coat.* He leans in, closer than comfort, sniffing. *That's no you been drinkin, is it!* Laughing, he lifts his hands from the handle of the child's buggy to mime shock. Mr Em remembers the afternoon and his neck aches. Perhaps, suddenly, not sober *enough* for this.

I don't think we've met, have we? he says, stooping to the child, and hears himself a ponderous buffoon.

Billy lifts his chin. *Brought her ower tae see the lights. Stays wi her ma, see.* Then, louder, *Paige, gie the Chemist Mannie ain o yer Christmas lollies.*

The child bends her small freckled face and inspects the plastic tub of lollipops on her lap, then removes a purple globe from her mouth and proffers it. Mr Em takes it carefully by the stick. *Thank you very much*, he says. *Merry Christmas, Paige.* He looks up at Billy B, smiling.

The Enemy Within

KIRSTIN ZHANG

Akbar scuffed at the dry soil with his sandals. They were in for another drought. Peanut plants drooped in the heat. The fruit on the pawpaw trees hung low on the skinny trunks, reminding him of the worn village women of his youth.

The dog that lay beneath the front step didn't even lift its nose from the dirt as Akbar made his way towards the house. He'd had a dog as a boy. It would follow every handful of tapioca from Akbar's bowl to his mouth. Without fail, Akbar would fling the bowl to the ground and shout, 'That look's enough to put you off your food.' The dog's thin body would flinch and then his stubby tail would wriggle in pleasure as it worked off the sticky scabs of tapioca from the inside of the bowl. Akbar wondered what had happened to that dog.

The old lady, who lived in the house, listened to him patiently.

'You don't understand,' he lapsed into the dialect of the area, 'it's a matter of life and death.'

He pointed to the poster stuck to the van. A giant mosquito caught within a rifle's crosshairs. Under it in red, 'Dengue: the enemy within.'

'One million IDR's not a lot to keep your family healthy,' he studiously avoided the gaze of the children with the sticky eyes who hung around her legs.

The official charge was less but so far no one had objected. It helped that the national radio station ran a continuous tally of the afflicted. You didn't need to read to know that already three hundred victims of the fever had been cremated, a thousand suspected cases had been hospitalised and there were now rumours that supplies of the chemicals used to destroy the mosquito nests were running low.

The old woman blinked towards the van. Her wispy hair was scraped back so that the skin stretched tight over her cheekbones. Knotted veins stood in relief around her hairline. One of the children sniffled.

Akbar put his hand into his shirt pocket and took out two pieces of caramel. Sighing, he held the candy out to the children. They looked at the old woman. She blinked with her watery eyes at Akbar.

'OK, I can spray for eighty.'

The woman nodded to the children.

They took the candy.

Akbar waved to the two men in the truck and they clambered out of the vehicle looking like extras from a western – bandanas tied around their faces to protect against the fumes of the chemicals.

As Akbar opened the passenger door, one of them, Jimmy, muttered, 'I wouldn't live in a dump like that, even if I was a mosquito.'

Akbar stopped and patted Jimmy's partner on the back, 'Hey, Tata, you're not looking too hot. Must be the fumes. Why don't you sit this one out.'

Jimmy began to unload the gear alone, muttering all the while.

Once they were both back in the van, Tata took out a piece of dried squid from the glove box and began to suck on it. 'So what'd you get?' he asked.

Akbar rolled down the window, 'I wish you wouldn't eat that stuff. It stinks up the van.'

He put his elbow on the window frame and watched Jimmy kick the dog from under the steps.

'So what did you get?' Tata repeated. He had started on a second piece of squid.

'Seventy,' replied Akbar.

'Seventy?'

Akbar fished a handful of crumpled notes out of his shirt pocket, took two for himself, handed two to Tata and put the rest into a plastic wallet at his feet. Jimmy got nothing; it was their little secret.

'We got Habibie tomorrow. We'll get plenty there.'

He thought of Habibie where the houses spilled out into bougainvillaea-filled gardens. Those houses belonged to people who could afford to run the air conditioning just for their Persian cat. The Philippino maid might offer him an iced coffee while the men sprayed.

The dog had sought shade under one of the paw trees and stood rubbing its back with its nose, pink and black mottled flesh showing through thinning grey hair. If his wife was in a good mood when he got home he'd ask her about getting a dog. He'd tell her that there was a rapist on the loose and he was not leaving her at home without proper security. He'd really play it up.

Jimmy was done.

The old lady and the children stood watching him walk back to the truck. The children waved to Akbar.

Hey, it could be true, Akbar thought.

He waved back.

There were a lot of bad people out there.

When he got home that evening, he found his wife mopping the floor and the contents of the fridge lying on the table.

'I'm going to my brother's,' she said as she pushed her feet into her shoes. She winced – her bunions were getting as big as onions.

As she reached the bottom of the stairs she shouted without turning round, 'And don't think I'm sharing a bed with a man who couldn't care less if I died of food poisoning.'

Akbar kicked the fridge – it usually did the trick – but the rusting heap simply shuddered and fell back into silence.

Akbar changed back into his sandals and ate dinner at the café round the corner.

On his return he found his wife already asleep. He pulled a futon from a cupboard in the front room and lay down without changing out of his clothes. But sleep was not restful. In his dreams giant mosquitoes hovered over a paddy field. Suddenly a voice from the dark shouted, 'Quick, spray the bastards now!'

There was a rattle of gunfire and mosquitoes began to drop amongst the rice plants.

'We'll never be safe until we kill them all,' called another voice.

There was more gunfire and then silence. In his dream, Akbar waited for a long time and then crept out from his hiding place. He felt the icy water creep around his ankles and then up around his calves. The dead mosquitoes lay face down in the stagnant water. He picked up a planting stick, which was floating nearby, and prodded one. The mosquito body bobbed right side up. It had the face of his father. Akbar woke himself with a shout.

'Is it not enough that I can't eat in my own house, but now you shout the place down,' his wife had snapped on the light and stood at the door.

Akbar sat blinking. 'I was dreaming,' he murmured.

His wife peered at him through puffy eyes. 'Dreams are for those with a guilty conscience,' and flicked off the electricity.

Unable to sleep Akbar got up. In the kitchen he made some barley tea and stood drinking it as he looked out through the mesh door. Outside a few people moved about like spectres in the grey light of early morning. Draining the last of the warm liquid between his teeth, he glanced back towards the dark interior of the house and slid his feet into his sandals.

His work unit was a fifteen-minute walk from the house and lay beside a river, which came up from the sea. Sometimes salt-water crocodiles or even basking sharks could be seen floating along amongst the tall weeds. Akbar was halfway across the bridge when he saw something sitting at the far end, just where the walkway split into two, one following the bank towards the main mosque and the other leading up to the back gate of his work place – the City Health and Cleansing Department. As he got closer, he realised that it was a large cardboard box. People were always dumping garbage here. He slid one of his hands into a slot in the side of the box, aiming to fling it into the nearest skip, and felt the contents move with a surprising weight. Laying the box back down, he opened it slowly. Tata had once found a boa constrictor asleep in a bucket under a house they had sprayed. Inside the box lay three puppies. At first glance all three seemed dead, but as Akbar stared down at them, one stuck out a little pink tongue and began to make a sucking movement. Akbar quickly folded down the flaps of the box again and carried it through the gates and into the yard of the Health and Cleansing Department. Only the man who worked the furnace was around at this time so Akbar knew he wasn't likely to meet anyone.

He left the box in a small storeroom behind the toilet block and went to look for some gloves. After disposing of the two dead puppies, he thoroughly checked the remaining one for ticks and fleas. It seemed remarkably clean. He took off the gloves and ran his fingers over the black fur. The puppy opened its eyes and peered at him. Its little mouth began to move again.

'We need to get you some food little man.'

In the canteen he found the remains of a carton of soya milk. He dripped this into the tiny mouth.

By the time he had finished feeding the puppy and had fashioned it a bed of torn newspaper, it was six o'clock. He ran his hand over the soft fur one more time and then shut the door to the storeroom behind him.

'You look like shit,' Tata stood slurping rice porridge in the canteen. 'Sleeping alone again?'

Akbar poured a glass of coffee and sat down at a table.

'Not eating?'

Akbar shook his head.

'After Habibie you'll be able to get the old lady her fridge, eh?'

Akbar quickly looked around to see if there was anyone else about and threw Tata a look.

'Talking of marital strife,' continued Tata between mouthfuls of porridge, 'Did you hear about the man who strangled his sixteen-stone wife and then tried to commit suicide by cutting off his penis? Front page of the *Daily*.'

Akbar sat nursing his coffee as Tata went back up for more porridge. He wondered why the man had chosen to strangle his wife. Surely there were easier ways to kill a woman – with insecticide for one.

Tata returned with more porridge and a plate of pickles. 'Can you imagine cutting off your penis?'

Akbar could not.

'The *Daily* said it was obviously a protest at the emasculation of men today.'

Akbar would have smiled, but he felt suddenly weary. He laid his head on his folded arms. His brother-in-law worked for one of the big pharmaceutical companies – in sales – that supplied chemicals to the Health and Cleansing Department. He had used his contacts to get Akbar a job nearly ten years ago. Before that Akbar had sweated from one manual job to the next. On a building site no one was interested in where you had come from.

'Come on sleeping beauty,' Tata slammed the table with his open palm and made Akbar jump. 'We got to go get those bloodsuckers – before they get us.'

On the way back to the department from Habibie, Akbar asked Tata to make a quick detour. They pulled up outside a well-known discount warehouse and Akbar spent fifteen minutes looking at fridges.

Jimmy who always carried a transistor with him sat in the back shaking his fist in time to the beat.

'Going to keep that down,' Akbar nodded as he clambered back in to the van, 'I got a real bad head.' He laid his cheek against the window. The glass was hot and he could feel the boom, boom, boom of the blood coursing through his brain. He wondered when he'd get a chance to check on the dog. The metal louvres were open in the storeroom but the heat was stifling today.

* * *

Tata and Jimmy immediately prepared lunch on return to the office; great bowls of cold noodles in a broth with a thick skin of fat and fine sliced green onions. Akbar felt sick and went to sit in the toilet. The old ceramic bowl was cool against his skin. He flicked through a newspaper that someone had left on the floor. It was mostly about the fever. There was also coverage of the upcoming elections. He was scanning the list of candidates when his eye caught an article about the return of the communists to the political fray.

The ghost of '65 still haunts many, but Indonesians must accept all its brothers if they are to enjoy a democratic and pluralistic society.

Akbar heard the flap of rubber slippers in the corridor and then recognised the legs of Tata from under the door. Tata rocked to and fro creating little pockets of air between his meaty soles and the rubber. Now and then these escaped in tiny gasps. There was then the sound of a steady stream against porcelain.

Suddenly Akbar felt as if someone had poured a bucket of ice water over his head and let out a groan.

'You in there, Akbar?'

With effort Akbar managed to reply, 'Stomach cramp.'

'What you need is good home-cooking,' Tata answered, 'the sooner you get that new fridge the better.'

After ten minutes the cramp had eased off. His hair was damp around his temples and he doused his face with cool water from the sink. When he left the toilets he turned towards the storeroom. Most of the men were having lunch and he might not have another chance to check on the puppy before it was time to head home.

* * *

The puppy began to make a gentle kind of whistling noise when it heard the door.

'Do you want to get us into trouble?' Akbar whispered.

He lifted the puppy out of the box and sat down on the floor. Beneath him the cement was cold and he shivered.

'We're going to have to find you a better home than this.' The tiny dog buried its nose into Akbar's lap. Perhaps he could get an allotment and keep the dog there. There were places you could rent further along the river. He knew his wife would never allow a dog into the house and there was no garden in which to put a kennel.

Maybe he'd think about it later; his head had begun to pound again. He flicked his tongue over his top lip. Akbar had never really been ill in his life but he had cheated death.

As a boy his family, like most peasants, were members of the Communist Party. After the failed coup of 1965, Su Harto's army had swiftly retaliated. As a regional party representative, Akbar's father had been taken away immediately. When news emerged that one of the daughters of one of the kidnapped generals had been killed during the débâcle, the army came back looking for younger blood. Akbar had hidden amongst the thin plants and ice water of the paddy. As the soldiers approached the house the dog had begun a ferocious barking. In Bali, a barking dog warned of the presence of evil spirits and, perhaps superstitious, the soldiers backed off and left. Shortly afterwards, Akbar had left too and for the past forty years, the truth had been hidden so deep within him that it was like an enemy banished to the most secure dungeon.

Beads of sweat were beginning to gather in the folds around his nose and around the creases of his mouth. The dog had wriggled along Akbar's legs and was nearly at his ankles. Akbar leant forward to retrieve the dog and suddenly felt himself falling into a faint.

Tiny as the little dog's whine was, it was enough to lead Tata to him when Akbar failed to return from the toilet. It was two o'clock and they were due to head out on another job. Akbar lay delirious from the dengue fever, muttering about giant mosquitoes and 'killing the bastards before they got you.'

When he opened his eyes he found Tata sitting beside the bed.

'It's just as well I can keep a secret.'

Akbar tried to speak but his tongue hung loose against his lips.

'What do you think your wife would say if she knew?'

'His wife knew what?' Akbar's wife materialised beside them.

'New fridge,' he managed to mumble.

Akbar's wife looked at Tata.

'He's ordered you a new fridge,' said Tata.

Akbar's wife almost smiled. She leant against the wall taking the weight off her swollen feet and began to suck contentedly on the can of iced coffee she had taken from her bag.

Akbar groped at the cotton sheet and pulled it further up around his neck.

Tata bent his head to say goodbye and whispered, 'I'll take care of the little matter till you're fighting fit and ready to take on the enemy again.'

He pointed his fingers towards a poster on the wall warning about the dengue and discharged two imaginary pistols.

AUTHORS' BIOGRAPHIES

John Aberdein was a herring fisherman and scallop diver, and is now a supply teacher and energy researcher for the SSP. His story 'Moving' was a runner-up in last year's *North* competition. His first novel *Amande's Bed* is launched this spring, while his second *Icarus 68* is on the stocks.

Andrew Alexander was born in 1974 and was brought up in the North-east of Scotland. He was educated at Glenalmond College, Perthshire, and at St John's College, Oxford. He now lives and works in Edinburgh and is currently completing his first novel, *Eagle*, a black comedy.

Thomas Brackenbury, a retired civil servant, has, for 30 years, divided his life between the Highlands and Edinburgh – having duty and family in both. He values family, privacy and seafood tagliatelle nere from *Paperino's* on Sauchiehall Street. 'Outside Broadcast' is the first of his works to be published.

Ewan Gault was born in 1981. He studied English Literature at Glasgow University and is returning there to do a Masters in Creative Writing. He is from Dollar, Clackmannanshire, but has spent the last year teaching in northern Japan. This is his first story to be published.

Joanna Lilley has a Masters degree in Creative Writing from Glasgow and Strathclyde Universities and has had several poems and short stories published, including in OpenInk's *A Fictional Guide to Scotland*. She has also written two novels. Her contribution to *Secrets* was inspired by her niece.

Nicolas McGregor was born in Kirkcaldy, Fife, in 1974 and studied English at Stirling University, and later, Information Technology. 'The Martha Day Affair' is his first published work. He currently live in Glenrothes in Fife, where he splits his time between reading, writing and playing online poker with an optimism that far outstrips his playing ability.

Lynda McDonald was born in Lincolnshire. She taught in Tower Hamlets, then moved to Edinburgh in the 1970s, where she worked in special education for a number of years. She has published short stories and poetry. Lynda completed an M.Phil in Creative Writing at Glasgow University last year and has recently finished her first novel.

Lesley McDowell has just completed her first novel, *The Elected*, about the relationship between Claire Clairmont and Mary Shelley. She has been a literary critic for a number of publications for seven years; before that, she completed a PhD on James Joyce and worked as an academic at St Andrews University.

Anne Morrison was born in the Western Isles in 1969 and has lived most of her life in the Highlands and Islands of Scotland. She currently lives in Sutherland, works as a freelance copywriter and runs a croft with her partner. She has two children and a large extended family.

Sylvia G Pearson began, at 55, to write short stories. Travel in South Africa and life in Shetland inspired her work, which has been published in several anthologies and has won prizes. She is currently working on a South African novel, a Shetland one, plus an early childhood memoir. She lives in Edinburgh and is the proud mother of two sons, her keenest critics and supporters.

Derek Robertson is from Renfrew and is 47 years of age. He is a commercial manager in the rail industry. He has submitted scripts for film and radio, written numerous short stories, and once thought of a novel idea for a novel. 'A Softer Devil' is his first published short story.

Frances Watt has a stunning view of the Angus side of the Grampian Mountains from her bathroom window. She has had some short fiction published before and has recently been writing for local community theatre projects – a high point last year was hearing performed in public a new song for which she had written the lyrics.

Kirstin Zhang, after a childhood in Papua New Guinea and studies in Tokyo and London, has settled in Scotland with her son, Laurens. Most recently she has worked with the Producers Alliance and Celtic Film & Television Festival. In September 2004 she won the Radio 4 Excess Baggage writing competition.

BIOGRAPHICAL NOTES

John Aberdein was a herring fisherman and scallop diver, and is now a supply teacher and energy researcher for the SSP. His story 'Moving'was a runner-up in last year's *North* competition. His first novel, *Amande's Bed*, is launched this spring, while his second, *Icarus 68*, is on the stocks.

Andrew Alexander was born in 1974 and was brought up in Inverness. He was educated at Glenalmond College, Perthshire and at St John's College, Oxford. He now lives and works in Edinburgh and is currently completing his first novel, *Eagle*, a black comedy.

Thomas Brackenbury, a retired civil servant, has, for 30 years, divided his life between the Highlands and Edinburgh - having duty and family in both. He values family, privacy and seafood tagliatelle nere from *Paperino's* on Sauchiehall Street. *Outside Broadcast* is the first of his works to be published.

Janice Galloway was born in Ayrshire. Her first novel, *The Trick is to Keep Breathing*, now regarded as a Scottish contemporary classic, was published in 1990. Since, she has published two books of short stories, the novels *Foreign Parts* and *Clara*, one opera and several poems. *Rosengarten*, Janice's collaborative work with the Orcadian sculptor Anne Bevan is now part of the permanent collection of the Hunterian Museum and Art Gallery in Glasgow.

Ewan Gault was born in 1981. He studied English Literature at Glasgow University and is returning there in October to do a Master's in Creative Writing. He is from Dollar, Clackmannanshire but has spent the last year teaching in Northern Japan. This is his first story to be published.

Joanna Lilley has a master's degree in creative writing from Glasgow and Strathclyde Universities and has had several poems and short stories published, including in OpenInk's *A Fictional Guide to Scotland*. She has also written two novels. Her contribution to *Secrets* was inspired by her niece.

Jackie Kay was born in Edinburgh in 1961 and grew up in Glasgow. Her most recent collection of poetry, *Life Mask*, is a Poetry Book Society recommendation. Her first novel, *Trumpet*, was awarded the Guardian Fiction Prize. Her collection of short stories *Why Don't You Stop Talking* was published in 2002.

Bernard MacLaverty was born in Belfast but now lives in Glasgow. He is currently Visiting Writer at Liverpool's John Moores University and University of Strathclyde. He has published four collections of short stories and four novels. He has written for other media – radio plays, television plays, screenplays.

Nicolas McGregor was born in Kirkcaldy, Fife, in 1974 and studied English at Stirling University, and later, Information Technology. 'The Martha Day Affair' is his first published work. He currently live in Glenrothes in Fife, where he splits his time between reading, writing and playing Texas Hold'em poker online with an optimism that far outstrips his playing ability.

Lynda McDonald was born in Lincolnshire. She taught in Tower Hamlets, then moved to Edinburgh in the 1970s, where she worked in special education for a number of years. She has published short stories and poetry. Lynda completed an M.Phil in Creative Writing at Glasgow University last year and has recently finished her first novel.

Lesley McDowell has just completed her first novel, *The Elected*, about the relationship between Claire Clairmont and Mary Shelley. She has been a literary critic for a number of publications for seven years; before that, she completed a PhD on James Joyce and worked as an academic at St Andrew University.

Anne Morrison was born in the Western Isles in 1969. She completed an MA in Religious Studies at Edinburgh University in 1992 and went on to work in economic development before embarking on a career as a copywriter. She now lives in Sutherland where she divides her time between writing and crafting.

Sylvia G Pearson began, at 55, to write short stories. Travel in South Africa and life in Shetland inspired widely contrasting backgrounds for her work which has been published in several anthologies, and has won prizes. She lives in Edinburgh, and is the proud mother of two sons, her keenest critics and supporters. She wishes to acknowledge a £6,000 award from the Scottish Arts Council, Edinburgh. Without this generosity, she would be unable to devote full-time energy to her writing.

Derek Robertson is from Renfrew and is forty-seven years of age. He is a commercial manager in the rail industry. He has submitted scripts for film and radio, written numerous short stories, and once thought of a novel idea for a novel. 'A Softer Devil' is his first published short story.

Ali Smith was born in Inverness in 1962. She is the author of several books including *Hotel World* (2001), which won the Encore Award, the East England Arts Award of the Year and the Scottish Arts Council Book of the Year Award in 2002. Her latest novel is *The Accidental*, published by Hamish Hamilton in 2005.

Frances Watt has a stunning view of the Angus side of the Grampian Mountains from her bathroom window. She has had some short fiction published before and has recently been writing for local community theatre projects – a high point last year was hearing performed in public a new song for which she had written the lyrics.

Kirstin Zhang, spent her childhood in Papua New Guinea. After studies in Tokyo and London, she settled in Scotland with her son, Laurens. Most recently she has worked with the Producers Alliance and Celtic Film & Television Festival. In September 2004 she won the BBC Radio 4 Excess Baggage writing competition.